ORANGE

is the new pink

NINA MALKIN

Point

To Gini and Rosie,

who know what friends are for

ISBN-13: 978-0-439-89965-9
ISBN-10: 0-439-89965-6

Book design by Alison Klapthor

12 11 10 9 8 7 6 5 4 3 2 1   7 8 9 10 11 12/0

Printed in the U.S.A.
First printing, July 2007

GOT JUICE?? Well, prove it.

Enter the Readers Run Amok contest and win a chance to spend the entire summer in New York City, working at your favorite magazine. And I mean working! Planning stories, running photo shoots, interviewing the hottest stars, and picking the coolest new trends — right here, at the preeminent voice of female youth culture. The girls who win will be the dominant force behind *Orange*'s first-ever Readers Run Amok issue. But I'll be here too — so we'll have plenty of time to bond while you guys produce the best issue of *Orange* ever! See page 137 for pesky contest rules and regs, and start putting together an application that'll set my brain cells on fire.

Luv & stuff —

Izzie

Isabel LaPointe
Editor-in-Chief

WHY I BELONG AT ORANGE
An Application Essay
By Babylon Edison

Family legend has it that I've always devoured magazines. Literally. Take the episode in my terrible twos when I got sick, so sick, violently sick, seriously unpretty. No one could figure out what would make a child *erupt* like that. Until my mom noticed tiny little teeth marks all over what little was left of her *New Yorker*. Oops! Sorry!

Not that I remember this. My first memory of magazine lust was *Garden Joy*. Don't cringe! I was seven, and in South Boston, where I'm from, it's cinder blocks and asphalt, not rosebushes and snapdragons. I'd escape into those petal-filled pages, wander through the colorful blooms, lie on the green lawns, inhale the perfume, butterflies and ladybugs landing on my shoulder — it was all in my mind, but absolute bliss!

By middle school I was fully over my flower phase but completely magazine obsessed. Every Thursday before recycling, the super in our building would give me my pick of the discard stack. I took it all: fashion and beauty, sports and entertainment, food, decor, travel, literary stuff, tabloid trash, even trade magazines for careers I couldn't care less about. The cool feel of glossy spreads; the way the layout tempted you, drew you in; how each magazine had its own flow, its own voice . . . it fascinated me.

My first year of high school, I turned conscientious rejecter and hated all things commercial — and what's a magazine but a vehicle for advertisements? So I started *Babyl*, my zine — as in my nickname, but also a clever homonym for babble, no? Putting it together was a blast, but *Babyl* was . . . limited, I admit. By me, for me, about me — a bit too much me, me, me . . . even for me! I dreamed of a magazine about girls like me and girls *not* like me, real girls, inspiring girls from across the globe who did all kinds of cool things. I craved killer content — straight-up articles about stuff that matters, that makes you think and feel. Plus, I wanted the whole package — awesome graphics and photography, a work of art you could carry in your backpack. And if it had to have ads, they should at least be for stuff I might actually consider purchasing.

Other magazines for girls my age? Most of them have been out since my mom read them. And no disrespect, but they're sort of silly and shallow and skinny-obsessed and boy crazy and girly and . . . in a word: *pink.*

And then: ta-da! It happened. Something better than

pink. *Orange*. Finally. Yay! *Orange* is the new pink, for girls like me — girls with juice.

I have bought, read, savored, and saved every edition of *Orange* since its launch. And since I'm obviously fated to be a magazine editor one day (if partially digesting *The New Yorker* doesn't say something about my destiny, what does?), I'd die for a chance to kick things off at the best place for girl culture on this planet. My title? Think! Editor, of course — the one who makes those mind-expanding, heart-exhilarating, and soul-stimulating real-life stories happen. I will work my butt off, make your masthead spin with brilliant ideas, do anything — except brew coffee. I am Babylon Edison, 17 years old from Boston, Massachusetts, and that is why I deserve a spot on *Orange*'s first-ever Readers Run Amok issue.

See you this summer! Whoo!

"I ABANDONED MY AWESOME BOYFRIEND!"

Why in the world would a girl leave a cute, cool, sweet, and so-devoted guy? No, her brain was not jacked by zombies....

Summer starts now, tonight, no matter what the calendar says. Here in Southie, the official summer kickoff is the first outdoor bash chez Quinn. Every neighborhood has one, a party house, and ours is the Quinns'. They've got the kind of parents who don't care what they do as long as it's done on premises. Any wonder their place has a gravitational pull on people? The guest list ought to top out at six million. Fiona and I are about to make it six million and two.

On the way there, Fiona's in a mood. The freeze I feel off her, I should have brought a jacket, worn jeans, but A) it's summer and B) it's a party, so a little skin — flirty top, denim mini — is essential. Besides, I know what's bothering her. I'm about to take off for the entire summer, and while she's happy for me — really, she is — she's sad for her.

For us: our foursome, Fiona and her boyfriend, Ben, me and my man, Jordan. Best friends, tight couples, the indomitable double date. With Jordan now the proud owner of a 1997 Volkswagen Cabriolet that actually runs, vacation was shaping up to be a whole lot of lazy — nothing to do, and a vehicle to get us anywhere we wanted to do it.

Only I had to go and spoil it all. I'll be spending the summer in NYC, living my wildest dream come true, thank you very much. Me, Babylon Edison, Think! Editor of *Orange* magazine. Sorry, but I am beyond ecstatic. Of course, there's no need to cram my excitement down Fiona's throat, so I try to defrost her by making silly small talk till we get to the Quinns', which we can hear bumping from a block away.

"Feena! Babyl!" If it's possible to holler listlessly, that's how Teri Quinn shouts us out. "The keg's in the yard — just push your way through."

It seems like Teri's already had a few, judging by how she hangs on us. I cut up a T-shirt for this event, slicing off the neckline to make it ultra-scoopy (pretty much the extent of my fashionista skills), and Teri's fumble moves it from sexy off-the-shoulder to embarrassingly off-the-elbow, pulling down my bra strap in the process.

Fiona scopes for our guys while I readjust my wardrobe malfunction, but I know Jordan couldn't possibly be here yet — he humps groceries at a fancy market in Beacon Hill, and doesn't get off till eight. Sometimes when we hang out, he comes by straight from work, but he'll want to shower tonight. He'll want to get close. Very close. Thinking of that,

I can practically feel-smell-taste him. I'm going to miss that boy so much!

With a nudge from Fiona I'm back to reality, and we wiggle through the sardine can of kids. The guy on keg duty teases us, asking to see ID; we roll our eyes and he pumps us foamy cupfuls. I'm taking it slow, sipping at the froth that tickles my lips, but Fiona gulps her beer.

"Oh, Babyl, I really do hate you," she moans. "I can't believe you're actually leaving. You are out of your mind, you know."

Much as I love the girl, I doubt I'll ever make her understand. Fiona's into *Orange*, too — we've both been subscribers since day one — but to her, working at a magazine might as well mean spelunking on Mars. When I decided to shoot for the Readers Run Amok program, I suggested she go for it too — being a total jock, Fiona would've made a great Move! Editor. Only she didn't even bother filling out the application. To me, it's a symptom of Southie — there's this pride of being from here, mixed with a dread that you'll never escape it, so you don't try. Unless you happen to be me.

But Fiona's upset, and I'm to blame. Beneath that bitchy exterior beats the heart of my best friend. She loves me, I know that; she just has to act tough, I know that too. Another symptom of Southie. Attitude is encrypted in our DNA.

"I never said I was sane," I say. "But you know I won't be

able to keep from calling you on a daily basis . . . or at least IMing . . . and, watch, you won't even miss me."

Does this sound convincing? I hope so, since it is pretty hard to imagine an entire Fiona-less summer. Before she can make a face or guzzle another beer or take off on an anti-*Orange* tirade, Ben and Jordan roll up to otherwise occupy both of us.

The kiss comes first. It's our ritual. He doesn't utter a syllable, just takes my face in his hands. Then that gentle yet insistent pressure of his mouth on mine, held for a few meaningful moments, says it all. Tonight, it seems to say more than ever. He inches away, still holding my face, and I reach up to touch his cheek. That's been our thing, our silent ceremonial hello smooch, for . . . wow, it's almost eight months now. First real crush, first real kiss, first real boyfriend — with Jordan everything always felt exactly right.

Of course, telling Jordan I got the gig at *Orange* — that I'd be taking off for two whole months — wasn't easy. It was fifth period. My lunch, his French, his custom to ditch French so he could be with me born out of Jordan logic. See, Jordan intends to be a cop — the McCormacks are a Five-O dynasty — and since he intends to join the force in Boston, not Paris, what does he need French for? Me, however, me he needs. And while ditching classes defies Babyl logic, I could live with him not conjugating verbs for a cuddle in the school yard.

"Uh-oh, what'd I do?" Jordan takes one look at me — staring through the chain-link fence, counting cars at the curb, cracks in the sidewalk, anything to avoid his true-blue eyes — and knows something's up. "Because whatever it is A) I didn't do it and B) I'm sorry."

Which one of us started that, the A) this and B) that thing? Did I get it from him, or did he get it from me? Doesn't matter — when you're a couple, in a lot of ways you're like one person.

"Nothing, Jordan." I forced myself to look at him, put a hand on his arm. "You didn't do a thing except be sweet to me," I said quietly, succinctly. The succinct quiet before the storm. "Okay Jordan look you know that thing in New York at *Orange* magazine well I got it all expenses paid and my parents are down and don't be upset Jordan please because it's only for the summer and I'll just oh I know how bad I'll yearn for you but this is going to open so many doors for me I have to do it —"

"Wait, whoa, what?" If only he had it on tape, he could've played it back slo-mo.

I dug in my backpack, pulled out the colored envelope vivid enough to make your mouth water. I took out the letter — more of a note, actually, casual, informal, friendly — and handed it to him.

Hey, Babylon!

Looks like we're going to be working together this summer at our favorite magazine! That is, if you can slog through the paperwork that's enclosed and send it all back by June 1st. You better!

Luv & stuff—

Izzie

Isabel LaPointe
Editor-in-Chief

"Wow," Jordan said when he finished reading. "Um, wow . . ."

I held my breath as he let it sink in. Then a smile broke across his face, and even though he had to coax it at first, once it was there, ear to ear, it was genuine. "Do you know how amazing you are?" he asked softly. "No, Babylon, do you know?" This is when he grabbed me and hugged me and kept whispering against my neck "Do you know? Do you know?" till I wasn't sure exactly what he was asking. But when he released me, he started in with practical questions, questions I could answer.

"When do you leave?"

"July first."

"How are you getting there?"

"They're flying me in!"

"Where will you stay?"

"In the NYU dorm — the Readers Run Amok program is hooked up with their School of Journalism somehow."

Then the sweetest, most wonderful, most Jordan question of all: "Can I come down and visit you? Take a long weekend? You could show me New York!"

"Of course! That would be so great! Of course, of course, of course!"

Throwing my arms around him, I knew in that instant how magical it all was. The best guy ever, the best summer ever, and the alarm clock wasn't about to buzz me out of it. It was true, it was real, it was happening for me.

Tonight I have to focus on Being Here Now. After all, this is sort of my bon voyage party, and now that our guys are here, Fiona's mood is vastly improved. It's a beautiful night — cloudless and crescent-mooned. Since the Quinns never take down their Christmas lights, the backyard is illuminated just enough to make everyone look good. Jordan especially — his sandy hair and easy smile, the start of a tan across his swim-team shoulders. Music blasts, a lively mix. Everybody's busting loose, the freedom of summer a fever.

I'm doing my level best to catch it. Yakking with the girls. Hamming it up for a camera. Taking a swig from a bottle of truly nasty stuff, like breathing fire in reverse — so that's tequila. Now I'm letting Jordan propel me into a corner of the yard where the Christmas lights have conveniently flickered out, and I'm pulling him to me just as much as he's pressing against me. I'm giggling into his mouth as we kiss our special kisses and, as our hands wander, I feel as hot for him as I did the first time we touched. Yet just as I'm ready to completely surrender to the insistent sensations, I'm tugged by a portion of my brain that is not Being Here Now but Being Someplace in the Imminent Future. It's awful but . . . I'm multitasking: Making out with my boyfriend while planning what I'll say when I meet Izzie LaPointe.

Soon as I start feeling a little guilty, as if I'm betraying Jordan by letting my thoughts run free as much as my hands and my lips, some girl I barely know comes stumbling over to the oak tree we're getting busy against, doesn't even bother with an excuse me, and loses her lunch a few inches away. That's when the banality of Southie reality hits me. And all I want, all I need, is to be is out of here.

HOW TO TALK TO STRANGERS

Yeah, your mom told you not to, but some-times a girl's got no choice. . . .

Before I know it I *am* out — up and out. Jetting out of Logan on the Delta Shuttle with all these businesspeople, me in my T-shirt, Jack Purcells, and ancient security-blanket jeans, my brick-colored hair in Bantu knots and my chin breaking out with a chain of sebaceous gland islands. Believe it or not, it's my first time on a plane. I'm not afraid of flying, not at all. I'm afraid of taking off, though — this I realize as I clutch the carpeted armrests and watch the world diminish through a window the size of a lunchbox. And as the captain announces our descent into New York, I discover I'm afraid of landing too.

How much of these newfound fears are rational concerns about velocity and thrust, and how much of them are wrapped up with emotions — what I'm taking off from, what I'm descending into — I have no clue. Fortunately Jordan and I parted on a positive, with his promise to visit planted in my brain and the taste of his good-bye kiss lingering on my lips. Still, there are so many *levels* to everything — literal meaning, deeper significance, subtle, subconscious connotation. Pondering this would be fine if I were on my way to Istanbul, but it only takes forty minutes to get to NYC by air and I don't have much time to muse.

I'm here.

Creeping down the aisle, following the signs to baggage claim. There aren't too many people jostling for position by the metal carousel — I guess shuttle regulars only pack a briefcase. I haul off my half-ton backpack detailed with band names and slogans drawn in Wite-Out and the humongous hard-sided suitcase I believe my mom inherited from *her* mom. Funny, though, I don't even think: now what? I'm more or less on automatic as I move toward the exit. Some men in rumpled suits gather at the exit holding cards, and a small, hunched one has a card that reads EDISON.

As in me? Yes, I decide, the hobbit is my driver, and I hand off my cumbersome bag. He hoists it easily — he's a pro — and leads me outside to a dark, shiny Lincoln. He slings my suitcase into the trunk, opens the door for me. He hasn't uttered a peep.

Which is cool. Who needs small talk? I'd rather think, drink in my first impressions of New York City. Except throwing my pack into the backseat almost leads to injury — someone is apparently sharing my ride, and I nearly clobber her with my bulging bag. I gasp out loud, but she doesn't

14

shriek or shrink or even blink, just tilts her head slightly as we check each other out.

I'm sharing my ride with a princess. The sort of girl who's accustomed to being chauffeured around in fancy cars, if not horse-drawn gilt-trimmed carriages, or parade floats laden with flowers — a sash across her chest and doing the royal wave. A modern-day fairy-tale protagonist in a white eyelet sundress ruffled at the neck and hem. Sandals that seem to be sewn out of daisy petals. Strawberry-golden hair spilling over milky shoulders and cornflower-blue eyes and sculpted carnelian lips and a porcelain complexion and yes, I am well aware I'm using every cliché in the book but that's her. Seated with her legs crossed at the ankle and her wrists crossed in her lap, she radiates against the dim leather recesses of the car. And me in my ultracasual gear, feeling hopelessly fashion challenged.

The princess speaks: "Hello." Just one word but it's like tapping a silver spoon against a crystal goblet. And when she speaks she smiles, and when she smiles her teeth sparkle. No, really.

I find it impossible to reply, because I am so not expecting this. Not that I mind company. Hell, if I was home I'd be crammed into Jordan's Volkswagen with about seven other kids right now.

"It's nice to meet you, Babylon," the princess says, her

voice like something you'd put on top of pancakes. "That's such a lovely name."

"Thanks." Ah, yes, verbal acuity — it's all coming back to me. I wonder how she knew me till I realize the hobbit must have told her who she was waiting for. Among my latest info package from *Orange* was a list of the other winners' names, but I don't know which one the princess is. "So who are you?" Soon as it's out my mouth I want to take it back — I don't mean to sound uncouth, but I bet it comes out that way.

"Please forgive me," she replies. "You probably didn't expect to be sharing the ride."

Ah, a princess *and* a clairvoyant.

"It's simply that my plane got in moments before yours, so I suppose they decided to send one car," she says. "Greener that way. It certainly doesn't bother me."

"Me neither!" I sputter. "I was just thinking what a colossal waste of fossil fuel when I saw that herd of Lincolns in the parking lot."

The princess laughs, and it's the sound of several very small bells pealing at once. "A herd of Lincolns," she says. "That's very well put. But where are my manners? I haven't introduced myself. I'm Emmalee . . . Emmalee Roberts."

Now, she actually extends her hand. Like who shakes hands? Apparently, Emmalee Roberts. So I reach over, take this slip of alabaster with a pulse, and we smile at each other.

There it is, the Empire State Building! We're cruising toward the city, nothing much outside the tinted windows to inspire awe, when suddenly it comes into view, that enormous Manhattan monument, the colored lights on the tower hazy against the dusk. Emmalee Roberts, miniature paragon of sophistication, may be right there next to me, but I can't contain my enthusiasm. "Whoa! That's it — the Empire State Building!" I say.

"Breathtaking, isn't it," Emmalee says, her validation surprising me. "Nothing like that on our Houston skyline." That's where Emmalee's from, Houston, though something tells me a hitch at some preparatory academy stomped most of the Texas twang from her dulcet tones. Emmalee will serve out the summer as Stun! Editor — that's the title *Orange* gives the style and beauty boss — and what makes my Respect-O-Meter tilt way over in her favor is the fact that the flouncy little frock she wears is her own creation, made out of curtains her mom was about to trash during a redecorating blitz. "Personally, however," she opines, "I prefer the Chrysler Building."

"Oh, yeah?" I'm about to ask which one that is when it becomes obvious — the slimmer, smaller structure to the right, an elegant, feminine building all done up in a pattern of icy white lights. "Makes sense," I say, nodding. "It looks like something you would wear, like a dress you'd design."

Emmalee treats me to her sparkling smile. "Babylon, truly? Do you mean it?" she says, glowing. "That may just be the nicest compliment I ever received."

I proceed to impart a crucial fact: "One thing you should know about me, Emmalee, I don't blow smoke."

"That *is* good to know," she says seriously, furrowing her brow. "Because, you see . . . I've spent time in New York, and much as I adore the place . . ." Now it's her turn to search for words, her gaze flitting toward the encroaching skyline. "People here . . . some of them . . ." She looks at me directly again. "Some of them are so full of shit."

Really, that's the last thing I expected to hear come out of her mouth, so my chin drops like the hinges are broken. Then I break out into the biggest grin — not over the "shit," but over the truth Emmalee uttered in no uncertain terms. Something unspoken exchanges between us then, and I come to the conclusion that I have just made a friend.

That's when the hobbit plunges into a tunnel, and we emerge on the other side, officially in Manhattan. Bullshit artists aside, this is the place where it all goes down. All the music, all the art, all the money, and of course all the words in all the books and magazines. My next breath is different from any that ever got sucked down my lungs before. It's as if those few minutes in the tunnel let me shed my Southie skin to adopt the dermis of a chick in charge at *Orange*. Confident, in control, and cool. I have *arrived*.

WHAT'S YOUR
FIT-IN FACTOR?

You're the new girl. Then again, so is everyone else. Is five-part harmony even remotely possible?

"Whoo-hee! Babylon! Emmalee!"

A tornado in three-inch wedges assaults Emmalee and me the second we hit the NYU dorm in Union Square, grabbing us into a double clutch. How this girl pegs us I'm not sure, but she acts like we're her long-lost cousins. Busty beneath a set of layered tanks, thighs like telephone poles under a miniskirt, large, flashing dark eyes, and a nimbus of bushy hair.

"I'm Tabby!" she tells us in a full-on down-south drawl. "And it's sooooo good to see you guys!"

Tabby lets us go, only to hug me and Emmalee individually. I'm no shrimp, so I submit to her squeeze with most of my dignity intact. Only teeny Miss Texas? Tabby's exuberance wrecks Emmalee's poise as it lifts her off the ground.

"Matumba, our chaperone — but don't call her a chaperone; ooh, she gave me *such* a look when I did — anyway, she went to talk to someone in authority," Tabby volunteers. "There seems to be some snag about our suite. And I don't know about you two but I sure would like to get to my room. My flight out of Nashville left at eight A.M., with a three-hour layover in Cleveland to boot — just about the most ridiculous thing I ever heard of." She flattens her lips at the incompetence of airlines. "But gosh, how about you all? Nice flights and all?"

Without waiting for our answers, Tabby flops onto a couch, yanking Emmalee and me down on either side of her. Finally a chance to absorb the lobby of the brand-spanking-new dorm. So far, so cool — a vast, clean space with long windows. Tile floors and sleek columns, bulletin boards decked with colorful flyers, comfortable couches and chairs arranged around tables. Kids everywhere — some striding briskly, others in clusters, hanging out, making plans. Even though they're college students and I've just finished my junior year in high school, I consider the playing-field level, if not slanted in my favor. After all, how many of *them* start work tomorrow at a major national magazine?

Still, they do look older. Every other guy sports some variation on facial hair, and the girls exude this meticulously casual vibe, whether the style statement is punk or boho or torn from the pages of *Vogue*. Maybe it's not the way they dress that makes them seem so mature, but the laconic ease they all seem to share, as if streaming from summer classes to internships to part-time money gigs to barhopping is one long smooth sloop sail.

"Sincowicz!" A black girl with a sleek, relaxed bob and a harried expression marches up to us. "Oh, so you got here." She consults some papers — our dossiers, no doubt. "Edison?" she narrows a glance at me. "Roberts?" she turns to assay Emmalee. We both nod, but I have to wonder if I've stumbled into boot camp. "I'm Matumba Knight," she says. "I'm an intern at *Orange,* so you'll be seeing me plenty. Okay, here's the deal. Due to a processing error, you won't be staying here at Union Square, but they found room for you in the Grand Street facility."

Am I obliged to salute or something? "Come on, get your shit together; we're getting on the subway," Matumba says, reveling in her boss-lady role. She consults her papers again and pulls out a cell phone to start making calls — as far as I can assess, she's giving our updated coordinates to the two *Orange* editors still in transit from the airport. (I'm just glad I made it here — since I don't have a cell I'd be stranded if I got here late!) Yammering instructions, Matumba decamps from the lobby; we follow behind her like displaced duck-lings. Emmalee and Tabby both have matching luggage, the heaviest piece on wheels. Unlike me, the geek with the clunky handheld hand-me-down. "Let's go, let's go," Matumba dictates, hustling us toward the subway. "We need to get to Grand Street before the rest of you *editors* get there."

Do I detect a hint of sarcasm, or is she just nasty by nature? I can't be deliberating that, as I have a more technical hurdle to vault. As in the vending machines that dispense the subway system's MetroCards. "What's the delay — it's not exactly rocket science," Matumba huffs.

One machine over, Tabby literally gasps at the rudeness, and I toss her a quick sympathy glance. But it's Emmalee, waiting in line behind me, who actually steps up. "Excuse me, Matumba," she says, "but if we're terribly pressed for time, why don't we take a taxi?"

Got to give the girl credit for speaking up — there's definitely an iron defiance blended into all that genteel breeding. Matumba, though, is not amused. "Ex*cuse* you? Because, Roberts, taxis are for tourists and other people with more money than sense," she shoots back. "Real New Yorkers take the subway. Because real New Yorkers know it's faster. You'll learn."

We hustle through the cavernous station, a Medusa of passageways with such exotic destinations as Coney Island and Pelham Bay Park. When we next see the light of night, we're right in the thick of Chinatown, the sidewalks so clogged with pedestrians it might as well be downtown Beijing. "Just keep it moving!" Matumba orders. How can I? An aroma of garlic and seared meat lavishes my senses from the restaurants crammed together like crayons in a box, and I realize I'm about to pass out from starvation. "Here, come on, this is it!" Matumba announces.

Wait a second. This is an NYU dorm? Not a fleabag hotel? An image of my mom and pops having a fit flashes in my brain, and I slide a glance at Emmalee. If she's upset by the dingy squalor she's resolved not to show it. Tabby, though — different story.

"*This* is where *Orange* expects us to stay?" she complains to the lobby at large, with its beat-up furniture and ratty carpet, a few random students lazing over frozen coffees. "Matumba, I had complete faith that you would sort everything out — but this," Tabby gestures haphazardly, "this is, well, I don't know *what* this is, but this," her big brown eyes leapfrog around, growing bigger and more aghast, "this is . . . not . . . acceptable!"

Like everything else about Tabby, her voice is on the large side — and a Southern lilt can sound seriously strident cranked up on hysteria. Doesn't she realize this is New York, where grit goes hand in hand with glamour? I exchange a quick look with Emmalee — she's thinking the same thing. But seeing how Matumba would be glad to knock some sense into any one of us, and Tabby's volunteering for target practice, I figure I'd better play interference.

"Hey, Tabby, come on," I say. "This is only the lobby, maybe the suites are nice." I don't know if my attempt at diplomacy diffuses the situation, or if Tabby and Matumba are simply startled out of head-butting stance by what happens next. As in the girl who comes ollieing down the flight of stairs at the back of the lobby. She glides to a stop in front of us and heel-flips her board. "Yo, what took you so long?" she says.

Mmm-hmm, it seems all Matumba's barking and prodding, trying to get us to Grand Street ahead of the other *Orange* contest winners, was to no avail. One of them not only beat us, she's turned the lobby into her own private indoor skate park.

"Oh my God!" cries Tabby. "You're Nae-Jo Rodriguez!"

I recognize the new Move! Editor's name from the info packet — but why does she look so familiar?

"That would be me!" says the bronzed-skinned girl in cutoff shorts and a bikini top, the T-shirt over it slit from neck to navel to flaunt a taut, tattooed six-pack.

"Your Tang! profile was sooo cool," Tabby gushes.

Oh, sure, now I remember. A couple of issues ago, Nae-Jo made Tang! — that page in *Orange* devoted to girls nominated by their friends for being unequivocally awesome. I always secretly wished that my friends would write to the magazine on my behalf. Ha, as if being able to spell onomatopoeia is Tang!-worthy. If I recall correctly, Nae-Jo made the page after she organized a charity athletic event in her neighborhood and in the process wound up showing some macho skater boys what she's made of.

"Yeah?" says Nae-Jo, her grin exposing a gold canine tooth. "Then gimme some love, chica."

She and Tabby high-five, then hug, and Tabby titters. "I make it a point to follow sports, even though entertainment is really my arena," Tabby says. As *Orange*'s Amuse! Editor, she'll run the department that covers all the music, movies, books, anime, and video games a girl with juice must know.

"Rodriguez, good, we're just about all present and accounted for," says Matumba with a flick of her papers. "Once Locke gets here, which had better be any minute, we can get you settled into your suite."

Nae-Jo saunters up to Matumba. I get the impression that's how she'd approach anyone — Jake Gyllenhaal, Hilary Clinton, whoever — with a swaggery, arm-swinging strut, her jet-black ponytail swinging to the rhythm. "You mean Paulina?" she asks.

"That's right," says Matumba. "Paulina Locke."

Nae-Jo smirks. "Veni, vidi, vici, baby!" she says.

Matumba and the other girls gape at her. Looks like I'm the only one who knows what Nae-Jo means. Well, I really don't know what she means — but I do know veni, vidi, vici is Latin, a little phrase favored by Julius Caesar when he was racking up his empire.

"She came, she saw, she conquered," Nae-Jo explains. "Took her about three whole seconds to scope out this crime scene, zero in on some hot-looking film student type, and roll with him."

Matumba shakes her head as if mosquitoes invaded her ears. "*What* did you say?" I almost feel sorry for her. Almost. "You're telling me she was already here . . . and she *left* . . . with some *guy*?"

"Ding! Ding! Ding!" Nae-Jo claps her hands. "You New York girls, so damn smart!"

So much for starting my first day at *Orange* after a restful night's sleep. There's just too much we need to get straight. First off, the accommodation situation. There are three bedrooms, one open hangout area with kitchenette, one bath, and five of us — well, there will be five if Paulina ever shows up.

"Ooh, Nae-Jo, we've just got to be roomies — we have so much in common!" Tabby says, grabbing Nae-Jo's hand.

Huh? They've known each other exactly five minutes! Reality and Tabby must not have much in common.

"Of course, if you want the single, I'd definitely understand," she gabs on breathlessly, "but I've brought tons of new DVDs, and I've got the coolest portable player — it's got two screens and everything — and anything you want to borrow — you know, if you need shampoo or whatever — you can feel free. Mi stuff es tu stuff!"

Damn, I've seen week-old puppies that were less needy. But Nae-Jo shrugs. "Sure, that'd be okay," she says. "I shared a room with two brothers till I was eight." Then she slides a glance at Emmalee. "I'm no snob."

If Emmalee notices the dis, she lets it roll off. Part of me wants to ask if she'll share the other double with me, but I don't want to be pushy — maybe she would prefer the privacy of her own room. Of course, I have the option of pouncing on the single myself, and wouldn't that be nice to have when Jordan comes to visit. Only just then Emmalee turns to me. "Will you be my roommate, Babyl?" she asks almost shyly.

"You sure?" I say. "Because I am so ready to plunk this suitcase down and not move it again."

"Absolutely!" With that, Emmalee pilots her wardrobe on wheels into our room.

After a half-assed attempt at unpacking in the rickety dressers and shared closet, we convene around the takeout menus Nae-Jo finds in the kitchenette. Food, glorious food! Chowing down, Matumba and this girl named Janna — a DA officially stationed down the hall from us — tear their hair out over the whereabouts of our errant Create! Editor. They leave messages on her cell — threatening messages, cajoling messages, desperate messages. At one point they actually place a call to Izzie LaPointe herself, but the *Orange* E-i-C is also incommunicado.

"Check them out — they're really losing their shit over this," says Nae-Jo, not caring if Matumba and Janna hear her or not. "I don't see what the big deal is. Maybe Paulina just didn't want to spend her first night in NYC sweltering in this hellhole."

Sweltering it is. The AC in the Dorm of Doom is about as efficient as your great-grandma with a paper fan. The spicy Chinese food we ordered only adds to the sweat factor.

"Makes us look like the wuss platoon," Nae-Jo adds. "Ten-year-olds at a slumber party."

"Personally, I find her behavior immature," says Emmalee, patting her lips with a napkin. "Not to mention rude to the rest of us."

Makes sense to me. It's nearly midnight and our first night as a group — Paulina should be here. "I got to go with Emmalee," I say, careful not to slurp my lo mein. "I mean, what are we here for? To meet guys and run around, or put together a kick-ass issue of *Orange*?"

Tabby giggles and twirls a chopstick. "Well, both!" she says.

"I'm with you, Tabby," says Nae-Jo, helping herself to the rest of General Tso's tofu. "The stuff at *Orange* will be cool, but . . ." she aims her gaze at me, "where I come from, the street is *seriously* educational."

Oh, please. Is Nae-Jo nominating herself as Ms. Streetwise America? Insinuating that I'm some Goody Two-shoes? Trying to put me on notice, just because I'm the other "ethnic" girl in the vicinity? I look at Nae-Jo levelly, then opt to ignore her. For one thing, I am too tired. And for another, Paulina Locke, six feet tall, spiked green hair, and slightly tipsy, has just made her entrance.

GET YOUR POINT ACROSS!

Girls with juice know how to speak their minds, and make sure everyone understands where they're coming from. Find out if you have the skills — or if you need a crash course in communication. . . .

There's a mouse on the sink. It better be a mouse — that is, a full-grown mouse — because the alternative — that it's a rat, a baby rat — is not one I can accept at seven thirty A.M. I assure myself the creature watching me brush my teeth is just one of the charming touches here at the Dorm of Doom, and when I run the tap whatever it is takes off anyway. Then I hop in the shower. We don't have to be at the *Orange* office for three hours, but since I'm awake I figure I better grab the bathroom while it's free.

Something tells me two of my suitemates — namely, Emmalee and Tabby — will demand extreme primp time. My guess is Nae-Jo will be the opposite — low-maintenance, not one to bother much with girly machinations. Not that she needs to. I can admit the girl is good-looking even if she did try to push my buttons last night. Competition must be basic instinct to her — a jock thing. I don't get it. Celebrate

30

your fellow females' virtues and talents, that's my philosophy, and it's central to the *Orange* mission too.

As to the virtues and talents of Paulina Locke, the jury is still out. Way out. I thought Matumba would murder her when she strolled in last night, but our chaperone controlled her homicidal tendencies, seething, "I am not going to waste any breath on you! You'll answer to Izzie LaPointe tomorrow."

Long and slim in her ink-stained T-shirt, fingernails bearing remnants of polish she must have applied back in, oh, early March, Paulina shrugged to convey the full whatever. "Uh-huh," she said. "So where do I crash?"

Leave that to the self-appointed welcome wagon. "Hi, Paulina! I'm Tabby, and of course you met Nae-Jo. We're roommates!" Somehow Tabby mustered the energy to get off the couch. "That's Babylon and Emmalee — they're roomies too. So by process of elimination, you get the single." Tabby pointed down the hall.

"Cool," Paulina said, then yawned. "I'm a vegetable. I'm fried." She emitted a cross between a burp and a snicker. "Guess that makes me tempura." She heaved her backpack as if it held an anvil and started off to her room. "I'll try not to die of loneliness in there."

Now, I can appreciate sarcasm as much as the next girl, but that kind of blasé arrogance is no way to win friends. After all, we'd been waiting up to meet her. Paulina must have sensed this, since she turned to face us again. Letting a glint into her narrow, mascara-smeared eyes, she squared her shoulders and clicked the heels of her scuffed Docs. "For those about to Run Amok," she shouted, "I salute you!"

With that battle cry-cum-lullaby, we all turned in.

The one bummer about our first day of work at *Orange* is it's also our last day before the July Fourth weekend — and the *Orange* You Glad You're Independent extravaganza.

"It's almost too much of a tease," I complain as we gather around a pole in the jam-packed uptown subway car. "I just want to sink my teeth in."

"I know, me too," says Paulina, pinching her face. "I'm viral with ideas, but instead of getting started, our first official activities at *Orange* will be as pawns for some dumb promo party!"

Hmm, maybe Paulina *does* take the Run Amok program seriously, despite her reckless disappearance last night. But to trash the kickoff of *Orange* You Glad . . . ? It reeks of treason — especially to our Amuse! Editor.

"Paulina, that's *so* wrong," Tabby gasps. "You must understand how crucial promotional events like the party at Club Cargo really are. Things like that keep people talking about *Orange,* keep us hot-hot-hot. I bet everyone who's anyone will be there."

"Uch!" Paulina summons disgust, and I half expect her to spit it at our feet. "That's because this is America — land of the media campaign. You could be selling dookie on a stick, but if you market it right, the masses will line up to buy it."

"Hey, don't be dissing the American way!" says Nae-Jo. "I intend to have a fat endorsement deal one day, and me making bank doesn't mean I'm any less awesome."

Naturally I feel pressured to add my two cents — I'm the Think! Editor, after all. "Paulina has a point," I begin. "Look at all the crap kids buy just because some celebrity says it's cool. But bottom line, *Orange isn't* dookie on a stick; *Orange* is the real deal, and if splashy events help call attention to our killer content, what's the harm?"

Uh-huhs all around. Even Paulina concedes she's not opposed to free food and drinks. Only Emmalee refrains from comment. She's on another plane, or at least in another era. Today her ensemble conjures vintage forties "career gal" — crisp white blouse, dove-gray pencil skirt, T-strap platforms, her hair swept into a chignon, a touch of tangerine gloss on her lips. Me, I'm about twenty fathoms more low-key, even though I did break out my new capris and a cute top for the occasion. Just as I'm wondering if Emmalee's just lost in thought or really is ignoring us, she shows she's been paying attention all along.

"It's remarkable how you can all be so political before

breakfast," she says sweetly. "Personally, I've got such butterflies about meeting Izzie LaPointe I can't concentrate on anything else."

Which is, of course, exactly what we're all going through, our dialectic on mass merchandising in America merely a distraction. Good thing we're not so distracted that we miss our stop.

The Chelsea address of Kult Ink, the indie publishing company that puts out *Orange,* isn't some soaring high-rise but a squat, functional building that probably housed sweatshops back in the day. No fancy lobby — just a dozy security guard and a fluorescent-lit hallway leading to an industrial elevator. Waiting for our ride to the sixth floor, I begin to realize that *Orange* isn't the only jewel in the Kult Ink crown.

This dawning starts subtly. With a guy. Just a guy — albeit a cute guy, lanky and tall, longish brown ringlets, hint of stubble — oblivious to everything but the pulse of his iPod. Half a minute later, two other guys — equally scruffy-sexy — come along, and they jostle the first guy, who greets them without removing his earbuds. Then, this other guy — no, this *man,* thirty maybe, in a suit and tie and GQ-quality gorgeous. And now, *another* studly specimen, his blond locks still wet, dressed in board shorts like he rode a wave to work.

Look, I am by no means boy crazy. And besides, I'm

taken. But as these cuties congregate — carrying coffees to go, and backpacks, and guitar cases — I can't *not* notice. Am I staring? Ogling? Openly drooling? For safety's sake, I fixate on my shoes — one look at the other girls and I know I'll bust out in a thoroughly embarrassing giggle jag. Finally the elevator wheezes open. The fine assortment of youth and young manhood holds back. Ladies first! Ultimately there are ten of us in there, and it's a tight fit. Tabby presses the button for six and we begin a tantalizing ascent.

One of the guys gets off on the second floor. I feel someone jab me once in the ribs — Paulina? Or Nae-Jo? I could kill her! I'm going to explode any second!

The sexy elder statesman exits on four, and two more get off on five, making masculine hand signals to the remaining male — the original curly-top with the iPod. We all disembark on six and head for the receptionist — who also happens to be male, and kind of cute, if you like that apple-cheeked baby-faced look — and that's when the music lover decides to acknowledge our existence. "So hey . . ." he says, tucking his earbuds into the pocket of his jeans. "You must be the high school girls . . . the ones who won that contest."

He smiles. Shyly? Snarkily? Hard to tell. But something about the way he's sizing us up sets me off. "The high school girls?" I fume. "Do you really expect us to respond to that?"

His mouth puckers like he tasted something tart.

"In the future," I continue, "if you must refer to us collectively, please — call us the Run Amoks. If you're lucky, we might just reply."

Now his lips do something else — not a pucker, not a smile, more of a twist. "Got it. The Run Amoks. I'll remember that," he says and, still with that inscrutable smirk, turns down the hall to his left.

One of the newly christened Run Amoks pinches my arm. It's Paulina, beaming approval. "Friggin' brilliant!" she whispers hoarsely.

All I feel is light-headed — a side effect of my power surge — when the receptionist launches from his desk. Behind him, blown-up covers of Kult Ink's magazines — *Orange,* of course, plus *Plank* (sports), *Squawk* (music), and *RoundBox* (think an edgier *Maxim*). "Greetings, Run Amoks!" he says. "I'm Finney, I'll be your receptionist this morning, just one of my many duties as a roving intern here at Kult Ink. And if you'll kindly follow me, I'll escort you to the conference room, where your ten-thirty is about to commence!"

"I MET MY IDOL – AND ACTED LIKE AN IDIOT!"

What could lead a smart, articulate girl to blunder her way through the first impression of a lifetime? And who knew two feet could fit so well into one mouth!

A croissant, a croissant, my kingdom for a croissant! Some fruit or OJ wouldn't hurt either. Guess I was too nervous to grab anything before we hit the subway — besides, none of the other girls did. Now my encounter with Elevator Boy has left me hypoglycemic — but thankfully, Finney ushers us into a breakfast buffet. The conference-room table groans with carbs and sugars of every description, plus the essential caffeine. "I've been directed to invite you all to pig out," says Finney, eyeing a platter of Krispy Kremes with blatant lust. "Izzie and the *Orange* senior staff will join you shortly."

He doesn't have to ask me twice. I load a plate with berries and sliced melon, then choose from an array of bread products and spreads. The rest of the Run Amoks pile it on too, and we sit down together around one end of the rectangular table.

"Babylon, you've got the flirting style of a warrior," Paulina tells me.

Of course, I have no clue what she's talking about. "Flirting — me?"

Nae-Jo laughs — a frisky yap. "What else would you call how you handled that boy?"

"Not flirting, no way!" I'm embarrassed and a little defensive. "I am not a flirt! Never acquired the skill . . ."

There's a teasing spark in Emmalee's eyes. "What's the famous quote?" she says. "'Flirts are born, not made.'"

"I was *not* flirting! A) I have a boyfriend and B) even if I didn't, I wouldn't go for some arrogant, dismissive jerk, and C) I'm not here to hook up — I'm here to *work*." I would point out that if I *had* been flirting it would have been a fiasco, considering how the boy bolted after I schooled him, but just then the door swings wide and in walks Izzie LaPointe, flanked by the five editors who'll be mentoring us this summer. They're a diverse group, obviously adults but still youngish, dressed casually in jeans or swingy summer skirts paired with cute blouses. But it's Izzie who commands our attention.

We recognize her immediately from her photos in *Orange* and her regular presence on MTV, Chick-TV, and ESPN. The golden pixie-punk haircut, the brilliant, knowing smile, the sharp, electric eyes. And her figure — buff and exuding a healthy aura as if she began her day not with exercise in the

38

grueling sense but something fun, like a run in the park with Copper. (Every *Orange* reader knows Copper, Izzie's Irish setter.) Plus, she's the total package, complete with brains and drive and vision, and that special something extra called charisma.

Being around her, you can feel it — her confidence, her style, and also these quirky unique qualities that defy cate-gorization. Beyond that, she's . . . what can I say? She's Izzie LaPointe! So it's not at all freaky the way we simultaneously drop our food and rise as a unit — a thrilled, squealing unit — to swarm her.

"Hey! Yo! Come on, you guys! Chill!" Izzie can't subdue us till she sticks two fingers in her mouth and delivers a whis-tle piercing enough to hail a taxi in Outer Mongolia. "Whoa! What a welcome!" she says. "You know, I *told* the caterer: No crystal meth in the OJ, but what else could have you guys so amped this morning!"

Around her, the women of *Orange* chuckle knowingly — the senior staff, and us Run Amoks too. How audacious of Izzie to make a druggie joke in front of the "kids." But we can read between the lines: She doesn't see us as kids; she sees us as equals.

"Okay, guys, I figured we'd make this an informal meet-ing — a get-to-know-you session — so let's get started." Izzie takes a bottle of water and a seat at the head of the table, Tabby and Nae-Jo snagging the spots next to her with lightning speed. "Let's introduce ourselves, say a little something about who you are, what you hope to accomplish here." She sips her water and grins. "I'll start: My name is Izzie LaPointe."

Ha! As if we didn't know.

"I'm the editor-in-chief of *Orange,* the magazine I founded two years ago. I love this magazine because of the way it helps girls like you love yourselves to the next level. And I was juiced to start the Readers Run Amok program to put my belief in you on the line. Letting you run this magazine will prove to the world how empowered and capable teen girls are." She takes another sip. "Plus, I figured it would be a way to tell my senior staff to watch their backs, let them see what kind of editorial talent is coming around the corner to steal their jobs for real!"

Everybody laughs. Then Izzie turns to warmly recognize the girl on her left, unleashing our monologues.

"Hey! Yo! Hi, everyone!" The way Nae-Jo springs up and almost topples her OJ, it seems she's got a slight case of nerves going on. Who wouldn't?

"I'm Nae-Jo Rodriguez, representing Long Beach, Cali, and I'm here to make the Move! pages rock!"

Hmm, her confidence sure came back in a hurry!

"I'm here to prove how strong and powerful girls with juice really are. Maybe it's a Latina thing. I'm Chicano — Mexican-American — and while I'm super proud of that, in my culture women are still treated like it's the nineteenth century. We're supposed to be so *nice,* so *sweet,* so *obedient.*"

Good for her, I think. She's so passionate; she makes me want to stand up and cheer.

"So I'm on a mission to wipe out those roles. Mostly I'm doing it through sports, but my attitude too. I *don't* play nice, I *don't* play sweet — I am hard-core, and I play to *win.* And now that I'm here at *Orange,* I can really —"

Just then, the swish of the conference-room door. Izzie lifts her gaze to the intruder. "Yes, Matumba? What is it?" she asks calmly.

Hurrying toward Izzie, Matumba sweeps her eyes over us, her glare on stun. She leans over to whisper briefly in Izzie's ear, then turns and marches out.

Izzie stands up. "Sorry, guys. I really want to hear every single word each one of you has to say, but duty calls elsewhere," she says. "Please keep going, speak your minds, strut your stuff. I'll try to be back in a few — but don't worry, tonight at the party there'll be some big-time bonding going on!"

The meeting takes on a whole different flavor after Izzie's departure, like everyone mentally unzips. All the senior editors seem pretty cool. Marguerite, the Stun! Editor, jokes about how she'll be spending the summer getting facials and massages while Emmalee slaves away, and Berni, the bubbly

Amuse! Editor, goes around the table and hugs each one of us. It's uncanny how much she's like Tabby — but what do I know, maybe all entertainment types are big girls with big personalities.

Naturally I'm most interested in what my mentor has to say. A bony, intense-looking woman with a few flecks of silver in her thick dark waves and blue-tinged circles under her eyes, Natalie Helperin doesn't blab on about where she's from or where she went to college — and at first I think she's going to be about as fun as a barrel of oat bran.

"I never thought I'd work in an office, be an editor — I wanted to become a novelist," she says. "Then I discovered how much I enjoyed eating!"

She doesn't look like she enjoys eating, but I give her credit for attempting a joke.

"Well, I bounced around from one magazine to another, but I didn't believe in what I was doing till I came to *Orange*," she says earnestly. "Yes, Kult Ink gives me my paycheck, and Izzie gave me my job, but in truth I work for you — the girls who read *Orange*, rely on *Orange*, and are inspired by *Orange*."

Okay, I feel that. I like her. Phew!

Listening to the other Run Amoks speak is illuminating and inspiring. Emmalee talks about how stifled she feels by restrictive perceptions of beauty, that in her view, every girl is beautiful. Paulina draws a verbal picture of a stultifying

Iowa hometown, and explains how she's always been a rebel — her very first word was "No!" Tabby titters on about trying to find a decent bagel in Nashville, and how she one day wants to own an entertainment empire that's committed to bashing stereotypes and nurturing new talent.

With each speech it becomes clear to me that different as we seem on the surface — our backgrounds, our ethnicities, our individual style statements — we're all alike in one major way: We're outsiders. All of us. The textbook beauty constrained by her perfect looks, the Jewish girl from the Bible Belt, the small-town punk inciting mosh pits at square dances, the jock chick out to give male dominance a beatdown. And me, of course, half black, half white, striving my way out of a working-class Irish neighborhood. We're all a little left of center, never entirely understood, always compelled to explain or defend how we look and think and feel. And I can't help pondering if that — more than anything else — is what got us here, what makes us Run Amok material.

"Yoo-hoo, Babyl!" Tabby's bray jolts me out of my musings. "You want to talk to us, or do you intend to be an international woman of mystery?"

My cheeks flush as I snap to. "Oops! Sorry, everyone!" I get to my feet. "My name is Bablyon Edison, and if it seems like I was zoning out over there, it's just because I was thinking about how —"

At this moment, Izzie LaPointe makes her grand reentrance, the shiny fabric of her skirt rustling audibly. All eyes turn to her. Immediately I stop talking . . . and start sweating. Izzie reaches across the table to grab a cluster of grapes, then leans against the windowsill. She pops a grape in her mouth, chews it, swallows, smiles. "Babylon, yes?" she says, her close-set eyes on me. "I interrupted you. Please," she pops another grape, gestures with a wave. "Finish up."

Finish up? I'd just begun! But abruptly I forget what I was going to say, and gibber on inanely, something about being from Southie, something about my parents, all of it true yet all of it boring, idiotic nonsense. My one chance to make a great first impression on Izzie LaPointe, and I utterly and completely blow it.

EXPLORE YOUR PARTY PERSONA

Every girl has her own unique way to work it when the night is long, the music is loud, and the dress code is out the window. Now get this: The way you behave at a blowout reveals volumes about who you really are....

Five girls, one shower, the social event of our lives — the word "chaos" doesn't begin to describe the scene in the Dorm of Doom. Tonight's bash will mark the Run Amoks' debut into New York media society, so the pre-party mood is pure frenzy.

"Go, Tabby, fifty more!" Nae-Jo screams over cranking beats.

"Noooo! Please! I can't!" Tabby's panting heavily, her face purple with exertion. "You're going to give me a heart attack, Nae!"

Well, if she hadn't been whining about water retention, Nae-Jo wouldn't have volunteered to personally coach her through an aerobics routine guaranteed to sweat it off. And how could Tabby turn down her new best friend?

"Tough toenails!" Nae-Jo, unrelenting, throws an intricate series of kicks and jabs.

Whoever has the rooms below us must think we've got marauding elephants up in here. Especially once Paulina stomps into the living room. "Enough!" she howls, blitzing the boom box as if honor bound to be our arbiter of cool. "I can't tolerate this miserable excuse for music! Pop radio is the opiate of the masses — don't you know it's rotting your brains?"

Tabby grabs the opportunity to hurl herself onto the sofa, while Nae-Jo and Paulina square off to debate rock versus reggaeton.

"Who died and made you deejay?" Nae-Jo's question is casual, but her limbs still flick effortlessly at the air.

"Nobody," retorts Paulina, her acid-green hair gooped with gel and sculpted into a faux hawk. "And nobody will get hurt as long as you let me at this radio." All the way down at the bottom of the dial, she finds a college station with a fondness for old-school punk. "Lo-bot-o-*meeee*! Lo-bot-o-*meeee*!" Paulina screams as the Ramones spew.

Right about then, Emmalee appears in a baby-doll mini and staggering heels. It's the sixth thing she's tried on in the last hour.

Me, I'm cross-legged on the stained carpet, perusing the latest issue of *Squawk*. At seven o'clock I'll slip into the silky aquamarine number that suits my skin tone and brings out the flecks of green in my eyes. My nicest dress. The one that still makes Jordan all goo-goo-eyed, even though I wear it on every special occasion. Basically it's my only dress. So what? I don't emo trip over the small stuff, like what to wear.

As to the big stuff, like what transpired this morning in the conference room? I need to set that to rest. Izzie had no way of knowing I'd just begun to talk, and it's not like I lapsed into stuttering monosyllables. I did fine. Even Emmalee said so.

"The light is so lovely right now," Emmalee murmurs — to me, to herself, to no one in particular — as she gazes out the window. Then she props a mirror against the sill and excavates a bulging makeup bag. Barefaced, her pale hair rolled onto clip-on curlers, she looks beautiful. But it's as though blushes and shadows function as her artfully applied armor, a shield against the world. And as she fills in her eyebrows with deft strokes of pencil, I notice Paulina is riveted on her too. Paulina, her eyes like liquid granite, impossible to read. I can't tell if her stare is appreciative or envious or what.

Nae-Jo races Tabby to the bathroom and — shocker! — beats her, slamming the door. Tabby pounds on it, wailing, "You said I could go first! I need to shave my legs!"

The harsh guitars of Paulina's chosen station suit the strangeness swirling inside me. I've got butterflies, butterflies in combat boots. I'm psyched for the party, yet some pesky part of me yearns for Jordan and the haven of his arms. Well, it's been a full day — after the morning meeting, we toured the *Orange* office, went over the schedule for the weekend, and sat down for individual sessions with our mentors. A *full* full day, all right — with the night about to begin.

"Okay, girls, this way!" That's Peggy Huxley, Kult Ink's publicity director, aka the Run Amoks' wrangler. Since we rolled into Cargo — past the actual velvet rope — she's been herding us from introduction to on-the-spot photo op to . . . holy crap!

"Hey, hey, hii-yiii! Estée Carrena here at *Orange* magazine's Orange You Glad You're Independent bash, with the young women who are going to be running this amazing magazine all summer. Come on, say hi to all your friends from Chick-TV!"

Peggy angles us into a neat knot in front of microphone, minicam, and the ever-popular Estée, host of *Chick Chat.* We hoot and hey and whoo on cue.

"Ohhh, Estée! This is so cool! I love Chick-TV!" says Tabby, for whom a simple hello is never enough.

"Thanks so much! And Chick-TV loves chicks like you!" Estée enthuses. "So how does it feel to be at the helm of *Orange*?" She pokes her mike toward Emmalee, our most videogenic Run Amok.

"It's an honor, since *Orange* is such an important part of

our lives," Emmalee says with perfect poise. "This is incredibly thrilling for all of us."

"Yeah, and we get to be on Chick-TV too!" chimes in Nae-Jo, always ready to snag some spotlight. "That doesn't suck so bad either, you know!"

Estée flashes one more megawatt smile before flitting off into the crowd, camera crew in tow, to land some real celebs.

They're here, all right. My experience with clubs is rather limited (as in nonexistent) but I would say Cargo is big enough to impress but small enough to be exclusive. Plus, Kult Ink is springing for an open bar and ample amounts of red, white, and blue culinary artistry. So anyone who's anyone who isn't already in the Hamptons for the holiday is primed to party. Rachel Bilson, Hayden Panettierre. Models I've seen in a million glossies. That kooky Fuse Veejay who always wears a different wig. Fiona is going to die when I e-mail her the star-studded recap.

The males of the species represent as well. Guys who look like they're in bands, even if they're not in bands. A soap stud or two. An abundance of athletes, both extreme and mainstream. In addition to famous fellas and an assortment of random guy guests, it seems that Kult Ink's male employees have all-access passes as well. Not that I recognize anyone in particular; it's more that the men of Kult Ink have a certain look. Call it shaggy-sexy. Too occupied with life to bother with mundane stuff like regularly scheduled haircuts and visits to the Laundromat.

"Hey, isn't that AROD?" Nae-Jo says loudly.

"Ooh, he is H-O-T!" squeals Tabby.

Paulina offers an obscene opinion that I won't repeat verbatim — suffice to say that balls are involved.

"Girls, here please!" Peggy waves us over. I'm beginning to feel like a contender at the Westminster Kennel Club dog show. "It's about time you met Alden Beck."

The king of the Kult Ink empire has a shiny bald head, a beak of a nose, and big black glasses — yet somehow he's handsome in a powerful-older-man sort of way. Unlike most men his age at the party, he's not in a suit, just jeans and a pearl-button Western shirt. As Peggy makes introductions, Alden takes each of our hands in both of his. He seems to have been briefed, since he already knows a bit about each one of us.

"So, Babylon, you think the Red Sox have a shot this year?" he asks this Bostonian.

"Well, they're looking good," I say. "And my boyfriend, Jordan, has a voodoo doll of every Yankee player, so the Sox will have that extra edge come play-off time."

Alden throws back his head and barks once, "Ha!"

I can see the fillings on his wisdom teeth. Score one for Babylon!

We all make polite small talk, and Peggy nabs a

photographer to capture the Kodak moment. All this posing with bigwigs and random celebs is giving me a real taste of what it's like to be an E-i-C — Izzie always plasters her letter from the editor page with high-profile pics.

After Alden lopes off, I'm hoping to kick back and enjoy myself. I understand the purpose of the meet-and-greet, but this is a Run Amok joint, and we deserve to have some fun. Maybe get out there on the dance floor, show 'em what we've got. Oh, and a mountain of strawberries, double-dunked in white chocolate, is calling my name.

"You hungry?" I ask Emmalee.

"Famished!" she says.

Paulina emits her signature hiss of derision. "*Tsssss!* How can you two think of food with so many other yummies around?"

No need to stop the presses — it's old news that Paulina Locke is beyond boy crazy. Then, as if on cue, one of the yummies in question approaches; he's blond, buff, adorable, and . . . oh my God, he's Duncan Branch of *Unreal World*.

"You're Duncan Branch!" cries Tabby. "I absolutely *love* your show."

"Thanks, that's really nice — we try," Duncan says. His entourage hangs back as he directs himself to Emmalee. "Um, hey, hi —"

Wow, check out the stammering TV star, I think. Emmalee must make him genuinely nervous.

"Um, I'd introduce myself, but your friend already did that," he continues valiantly as Em looks coolly past his right ear. "Which is good, I guess. Because I really would like to meet you. . . ."

Emmalee lets her gaze go past Duncan's left ear. It's as though he doesn't even exist. I'd think she was totally snubbing him if she didn't seem so uncomfortable, as if scoping an escape route.

"Um, hello?" Duncan isn't giving up. He weaves left to right, working that boyish charm. Finally he succeeds in catching Em's eye.

Very softly, she says, "Pardon me." And, with a shift of her shoulders, she finds an opening in the crowd and hurriedly steps away, leaving poor Duncan dejected and confused — probably for the first time in his entire life. I give him a sympathy glance before darting after Em.

What was that *all about?* I wonder. Does she hate blonds or something? But before I can drill her, Peggy Huxley hovers around again to usher us through another bout of intros and photos. My questions will have to wait.

POWER UP YOUR
STAGE PRESENCE

In the big city, all the world's a stage. So when the spotlight is on you, you better beam back just as bright!

Half an hour later, we regroup again near the spread of food, and I think I'll finally be able to snag myself a strawberry. But no — not meant to be!

"Uh-oh, look out!" Tabby says, nudging me.

Oh, please, if it isn't Matumba Knight, intern of evil, making her way toward us. Worse, she's got her crew with her. But I shouldn't jump to conclusions — perhaps she wants to play nice.

"Hey, Matumba," I say. She's rocking a tiered skirt in some gauzy material and a halter top — a good look, so I toss in a compliment. "You look cute."

Matumba grimaces. "Oh, thanks," she says. "I thought you *editors* should meet some of the *Orange* interns."

That condescending slant on "editors" again! By now I'm sure I'm not imagining it.

"You know, in case you ever find yourselves roaming the office, completely clueless," she continues. "You might want to ask a question of someone who actually knows what's up."

A snicker from a busty sun worshipper in a clingy wrap top. A vapid expression from a pasty string bean sporting forty pounds of beads around her neck. All three girls clutch the exact same bag — leather, canvas, covered in logos, either bona fide designer or a reasonable facsimile, not that I could tell the difference.

"Sure, that's nice of you, Matumba." I refuse to so much as acknowledge her sarcasm. Turning to the too-tan chick, I say, "Hey, I'm Babylon."

She gives me a phony smile, all teeth and no soul. "I'm Angela."

I turn to the string bean, but before I can speak, Paulina takes over. "And you're Kaitlyn, right?" she says. "You probably know I'm Paulina. I saw you in Create! today."

I can sense Paulina's attitude rising. "You were really working that Phaser," she says.

Nae-Jo's either curious — or eager to fan the flames. "Phaser? What's a Phaser?" she asks.

"Oh, that's the color printer." Paulina's talking to Nae-Jo but treating Kaitlyn to her slit-eyed stare. "Kaitlyn's job is to make copies in my department."

Is that a smackdown I sense between the Run Amoks

and the college interns? If so, Peggy Huxley emerges to put the battle on hold. "Girls, quickly, this way, you need to get backstage, and I mean this instant!"

"Welcome, independent women!" Izzie LaPointe waits half a beat. "And independent men."

Watching her from the darkened wings of Club Cargo's small stage, I'm struck by even more facets of the woman's skill set: her impeccable timing, the way she commands the attention of a crowd. The dress? A bold, graphic print. The hair? Fluffed up a notch. The earrings? Dangling to her shoulders. This is how Izzie goes gala. For all her down-to-earth real-girl cred, it's clear she can dress up and play with the big dogs when she has to.

"I'm so glad you could all attend *Orange*'s Fourth of July jump-off." She stands just close enough to the microphone, her voice carrying through the club. "And I'm not going to drill you with details on *Orange* magazine's mind-boggling circ or how many ad pages we've gained in the last six months. All I'm going to do is tell you *why Orange* has the juice — no, I won't tell you, I'll *show* you, because what makes *Orange* kick ass is the young women who read it. Five of them are here tonight — they're the editorial team of our first-ever Readers Run Amok program. I know that once you meet them you'll understand why I have so much faith in the future of this world. Because these are the young women who are going to lead us there."

A small hand grabs mine, and I know it's got to be Emmalee at my side. "I could faint!" she whispers.

Squeezing back, I turn to give her a reassuring smile. Sure, it's awesome that Izzie's making such a big deal about us, but having to trot out onstage in front of all those people is the deep end of anxiety.

"I hear you," I tell Em. "But it ought to be over in a few, and then we'll be able to throw our hands in the air and party like we just don't care!"

Emmalee giggles softly. Then we hear Izzie announce: "Our Think! Editor — MS. BABYLON EDISON!"

She must be going alphabetically, so I'm first. As I walk rubber-legged onto the stage, I train my thoughts on the strawberries, like they're all that matters on the planet. Next thing I know I'm out there, the audience is clapping like crazy. Izzie's hugging me and smiling at me, making me feel like this whole rigmarole is completely normal and natural. It helps — sort of: Because the truth is, hearing the applause and basking in Izzie's glow is so amazing, it's almost surreal. Like I'm famous, although I haven't done anything yet; I'm somebody special because Izzie says I am. And nothing — not the glitterati thronging the club in their designer clothes, not the courtesy-of-*Orange* goody bags packed with makeup, jewelry, and DVDs — compares to that feeling.

Soon we're all onstage, clustered around our badass boss, who gives us one more collective shout-out. "Ladies and gentlemen, the Run Amoks!"

Hearing her call us the Run Amoks thrills me. Did someone tip Izzie off that I made up the moniker? Or did we both come up with it independently — an example of great minds thinking alike?

"These girls are truly incredible. They were chosen for their talents, for their drive and ambition and utter brilliance, and they're about to show the world what girls with juice can really do!" Izzie pauses to beam at us. "Guys, check it out: I wanted you to come up here so the powers that be in NYC can get a good look at you. But there's another reason. I have something to tell you."

Another of her momentous pauses. We all lean in closer, hanging on her next words.

"You Run Amoks will be busy producing the best damned issue of *Orange* ever, but that's not all." Izzie is sparkling; she's all lit up. I wouldn't be surprised if an electric current came zapping out of a fingertip. "One of you — the girl who proves to me she's got the most juice — will walk away from this experience with a little something extra: her own column in *Orange,* a page all her own, to fill with whatever words and images and ideas she wants, for all of next year."

The info starts to infiltrate my brain, and I feel my extremities tingle. The same tingle must be zigzagging its way through the rest of the Run Amoks. Our own column! Our own page! For anything we want! For a year!

But wait a second — I'm getting it twisted. Not *our* own page. *My* own page. My space, my forum, my readers. That would slam-dunk my journalism career, not to mention get me in to whatever college I want, but more important it's a chance to be a voice for girls with juice across the country. A dozen articles about issues I want to spout about. My own page!

Or Paulina's own page.

Or Tabby's . . .

Or Nae-Jo's . . .

Or Emmalee's.

One page. One girl.

I find myself blinking rapidly, trying to focus, trying not to fall off the stage. Around me, the Run Amoks respond accordingly. Tabby clasping her hands to her heart, Nae-Jo bouncing up and down. Paulina widens her stance and throws her head back like a superhero, and Em strikes a picture-perfect pose, her eyes and smile shining. I try to figure out what's really going through their minds. Easy enough. I know exactly what they're thinking, because they couldn't be thinking anything else. They're thinking what I'm thinking:

Let the backstabbing begin.

THE ESSENTIAL
ELEMENTS OF COOL

Designer bag (not a knockoff!)? Foolproof fake ID? Hundred-dollar T-shirt? Cell phone so advanced it has ESP? Find out what a girl really needs to achieve all-access status. . . .

Central Park, this massive slab of nature smack-dab in the middle of Manhattan, is the ideal venue for Trees Please! — a rally to raise awareness on the rampant rape of our environment. It makes me proud that *Orange* not only has a feature on deforestation in the current issue, but also sends us out to pimp the cause on the Friday before July Fourth.

"You guys look great!" Izzie psyches us up as we gather near the band shell, Got Juice! emblazoned across our chests and Trees Please! on the butt of our jogging shorts. "You're superheroes, here to show the world that every tree, plant, flower, bush, and blade of grass counts!" Our mission this early morning: To canvass the area, distributing copies of the July *Orange* plus literature from the Trees Please! people. And of course, pose for pictures with Izzie and all the environmentalists and politicians who've gathered.

So far, we haven't exchanged a single sentence about the bomb Izzie dropped on us last night. It was surreal how we processed her announcement. Jumping up and down, all gabbing at once but not actually saying anything. Then the music blared up again, and I remember Nae-Jo shouting, "That's my jam!" as we floated from the stage to claim the dance floor. Well, you know what happens when five chicks at the top of their game are ruling a room — can you say guy magnets? Still, the Run Amoks grooved as a unit, all these boys orbiting us like satellites. Imagine the stress of the last two days finally exploding into heart-pumping, booty-shaking, hands-in-the-air release.

There's another possible explanation for our dance-floor gyrations, however. We were already at it — exhibiting for Izzie, competing for the prize. The thought slaps me, but I put it aside. The Trees Please! rally is starting, and the rally, I remind myself, is about something critical — not some petty byline on a page, but the ultimate survival of every living thing.

"I cannot believe you left home without one!" This is not an American Express commercial; this is Paulina, incredulous. "How do you expect to *do* anything?"

We're heading back from Trees Please! and the subject of Paulina's astonishment is fake IDs — or rather, Tabby's lack of one. The rest of us are good. I got the hookup from Teri Quinn's older brother before I left Boston; designing and dispensing illicit licenses to the youth of Southie is his *raison d'etre*.

Tabby bites her lip, tries to make some excuse, but her roomie comes to her rescue before she can say anything too dorky. "Don't worry, we'll get you one," Nae-Jo says. Even though we're all the same age, Nae-Jo seems to have taken on the role of Tabby's streetwise older sister. "Although it may take a while."

"Yeah, *sorry*." Paulina has the most insincere "sorry" I have ever heard. That art-snob mystique of hers is starting to work my nerves. "No adult beverages for you this evening."

I bet Paulina already has a map of every hipster hangout in town. "Well, none for me either," I say.

Run Amok eyes bulge at me. Why — because I'm not hot to spend my first Friday night in New York getting wasted?

"I'm exhausted," I say. "I really need to call Jordan, and after that I just want to stay in and read."

Which is true. Basically. See, we'll be presenting ideas for our sections to Izzie on Monday, and I need to make sure my pitch is letter-perfect. I've got a killer concept for *Think!* — girls helping girls in crisis situations — but I need to make sure my research is on point, that the tone is smart, hip, unassailably *Orange*.

"Well, Babyl, if you're staying in, can I use your ID?" Tabby wheedles.

Did she really ask me that? Nashville must be the naïveté capital of the USA. "Tabby, that's impossible," I say as nicely as I can.

She gets huffy anyway. "Babylon Edison! Must you always be so selfish?"

Okay, I've known this girl forty-eight hours yet she's already an expert on what I'm "always" like? Fortunately Paulina breaks it down for her. "Tabby, do you even know what an ID is?" she says, cracking up. "Because it's not a letter from your mommy. It's a *photo* ID — and no matter how much bronzer you put on, no way you're passing for black!"

Pay phones are like relics of an ancient civilization — forget finding one that works. There's a pay phone on every floor of the Dorm of Doom, but only two of them function, and just my luck the other two people on earth besides me who don't have cells are perpetually yakking on them. Yes, believe it — I am cell-less. We don't have a lot of money, and I didn't want to put the expense on my parents — I was supposed to have a part-time job that actually paid this summer. Besides, I know me: I'm real responsible in some ways, but I have a way of losing things.

Yet now that I'm alone, the *Orange* loaner laptop open and all my papers scattered, I can't concentrate. It's a balmy summer night, I'm on my bed wearing nothing but a T-shirt and panties, and thoughts of Jordan are driving me to distraction. Where is he right now? What's he up to? Does he miss me? I shoot him off a quick e-mail, sighing when I press SEND. Since I've been away, he's gotten better about checking his account, but he's never been much of a writer — his IMs are frustrating, basically one-word answers. Unlike Fiona's. The girl can't spell to save her life, but she's keeping me up-to-date on the Southie social scene. I wait to see if Jordan's going to hit me back, then glance at the clock — it's seven P.M., he's probably still at work. Oh, well, even if he did reply, it wouldn't be the same as hearing him say my name.

Frustrated, claustrophobic, I toss on shorts and head out, wandering aimlessly. Before long, I'm in NoLiTa — that's an acronym for North of Little Italy, according to my NYC guidebook — all cobblestone streets and tiny, trendy boutiques. On a whim I venture into one.

"May I help you?" This skinny saleschick practically pounces on me.

"No thanks, just looking," I say.

There's something snide in her expression, but she doesn't chase me out — which compels me to browse. I pick up a T-shirt from a stack on display, nearly choking when I check the price tag. Who would pay ninety bucks plus tax for a T-shirt? Just then, a woman and a young girl stroll in. My French is good enough to ascertain that they're mother and daughter, Parisian fashion victims with euros to burn. I run my fingers over a few more astronomically priced scraps of fabric and duck out.

"Italian ice?"

It sounds like a magic potion, a cool and soothing salve. I smile at the man with the rolling cart. "You got cherry?"

"Cherry it is!"

Two scoops of compressed crimson slush in a paper cup. The intense flavor reddens my lips, lifts my spirits, and spurs my thoughts back to Jordan. When it comes to Italian ice, he's a tutti-frutti man. Is he savoring one now? Is he in the car? At the beach? Who's he with? It's maddening, wanting to be here on my own, and there with him, equally, at the same time. I tromp back to the Dorm of Doom, brush my teeth, exfoliate the city off my face, and lie in bed, contemplating the inside of my eyelids.

"Shh, Tabby!" I hear Emmalee softly admonish. "Babylon might be sleeping!"

"Oopsie!" Tabby burps, then giggles. "Ooh, I really got to go potty!"

Something bumps out there. "Be careful, Tabby!" Emmalee cries in a whisper. "Here, the bathroom's *this* way."

The next sound is Emmalee making a stealth entrance into our room.

"I'm awake," I tell her. "You can turn on the light."

She does, and I sit up. Her face is mix a of scorn and mirth.

"What up?" I ask.

Emmalee perches on my bed. "Restaurant waiters are incorrigibly negligent about checking IDs," she says. "If you think it's easy to steer a tipsy Tabby through the streets of New York, I assure you it is not!"

We trade grins. "Paulina and Nae?"

Emmalee shrugs. "Don't ask me." She blinks at the room. "We really need to spruce this place up. Are you up for extreme dorm makeover?"

"As long as we can do it on the cheap."

"Babyl, you wait and see," she says. "Give me a well-stocked ninety-nine-cent store and I'll transform this place into something *Architectural Digest* would feature!"

For a minute we sit quietly. I want to bring up the column — eventually we'll all have to talk about it — but I hold back. Em and I are becoming so tight, I don't want to confront an issue that could potentially tear us apart. Then Emmalee sighs. "I suppose I should make sure Tabby hasn't fallen into the toilet."

"Hey, Em?" I ask. "Can I borrow your cell?"

Without hesitation she goes into her purse and hands it to me. "Jordan?"

I adjust my pillow. "I just . . . it's so hard to get him out of my head. I need his voice, his encouraging words — he really supports what I'm doing."

Emmalee slips a nightgown from her dresser, then turns to me before she leaves the room. "Hey, Babyl?" she says. "I'm very glad you're here."

"Thank you," I say. "I'm glad you're here too." I glance at her bag, on the floor between our beds. It's the real deal, not some cheap imitation like they hawk in the stalls down on Canal Street, but what's cool is how Em mixes pricey pieces with thrift shop stuff and her own creations for her unique brand of chic. "So I'll just put the phone back in your bag, okay? I won't be on long."

"Don't be silly — talk as long as you like," she says.

Did I luck out in the roommate department or what? "Thanks!" I say. "Night, Em."

"Night, Babyl." She turns off the light on her way out. "Be sure and tell him I say hi."

I flip the phone. It glows to guide me. I tap the number my heart knows best. But my call goes straight to voice mail. Oh, Jordan — where are you now?

BOYS ON THE BRAIN

Studies show that the male of the species is a simple creature. So why do we devote so much time and energy obsessing over guys?

On the agenda for Saturday, the complete antithesis to Trees Please!. The Kult Kruise is a schmooze-fest on the Hudson for a select group of the company's advertising clients — with us Run Amoks along as test subjects for a slew of new products. It's like a floating R&D lab — R&D, that's biz-speak for research and development. Still, it's all very glamorous: beautiful yacht, dutiful crew, sun-drenched afternoon. We'll be giving our unbiased, unabashed opinions of sneakers, soft drinks, and other crap along with some male interns from *Squawk, Plank,* and *RoundBox,* and as the male contingent climbs aboard, I begin to comprehend why the *Orange* interns resent us. After all, if it weren't for the inception of the Run Amok program, they'd be the ones lounging on deck chairs and making "crucial" youth market judgment calls today.

"Here comes your boy-yee." Paulina taps my shoulder with a tube of sunscreen.

"Who?" I wonder. "Oh . . ."

With his curls tucked under a baseball cap, I don't recognize him at first. Elevator Boy. One of a half dozen clowning guys taking a seat among the clients, publishers, E-i-Cs, and us. Feeling myself flush, I study a fascinating new freckle that's appeared on my knee.

"Hey! The Run Amoks!" This is from Finney, the friendly, cherub-cheeked guy who welcomed us to Kult Ink our first day. "How's it going?" He addresses all of us, but as I glance up from my freckle it seems to me his gaze is glued to Tabby.

"Doesn't suck," Paulina answers. "Although I can't see how my career as an art director will benefit by serving as a guinea pig for corporate America!"

That girl has no sense of propriety at all, but Alden Beck ignores her as he claps his palms together for our attention. He asks our informal panel to introduce ourselves to the clients. "Say your name, your age — anything you think these captains of industry should know about you."

Round and round we go.

Until: "I'm Gabe Kandleman."

So, Elevator Boy has a name.

"I'm eighteen; I'm going into my sophomore year at Columbia; and I intern at *Squawk*. And I guess you captains of industry should know that the last time I was on a boat, I got seasick. So someone please tell me if I start turning green, so I can excuse myself."

Columbia, huh? And a sophomore at eighteen. My, isn't he an overachiever. Funny, too. I raise my eyes to check out Gabe Kandleman, Columbia student and comedian, in his Gumby T-shirt and baggy khaki shorts. He's got that inscrutable expression on his face, but thanks to his dark shades, I can't tell if he's aiming that snarky-smiley-sexy thing at me or not.

Fortunately, corporate America is intent on grilling us hard, so my attention is soon diverted. We sip a sea of juice, chew a ton of gum, and sample various hair gels. We comment on packaging and logos, debate various designs and slogans. Holy sensory overload! Then, just when I think I've maxed out, it's time for the blind sniff test.

"You've got to be in the dark, you see — or, ha-ha, you don't see!" says the man from Sterling-Meadows, a fragrance manufacturer, as he hands out sleep masks. "If you could see the guy you're smelling, it might affect your impression of the scent. So . . . blindfolds on, ladies, please.

"Now, guys, each of you will be given one of two scents to try on before approaching the ladies. All you have to do is, you know, mist yourselves lightly. Lightly! Not too much! That's it, that's enough. Great!"

Snickers ricochet all around me — the adults on deck evidently think this is hilarious — as, one by one, a boy approaches a blindfolded girl.

"Ooh! This is . . . this is . . . oh! I love this!" That's Tabby, going first.

Nae-Jo's not so sure. "I don't know." She takes another whiff, then tells her guy, "Yo, I think you're too sweaty already for cologne to work on you."

"My turn! My turn!" Paulina yelps. "Awwww, yeah! Damn, can I keep him?"

I hear Emmalee next, a consummate professional: "Musky . . . a bit tangy . . . it, hmmm, I'd imagine it depends on the particular guy . . . but . . . yes, on him, yes, I approve!"

"Good point, Emmalee!" says the Sterling-Meadows exec. "Here, wait. Sniff this young man."

"Ew! Oh my goodness, no!" she cries. "Forgive me but . . . insect repellent!"

Well, here goes nothing. Someone places my hands on a set of masculine shoulders to keep me steady. I lean in . . . inhale and . . . I'm overcome. My knees go weak. Whatever's in the scent mixes with molecules inherent to this boy's body chemistry to create something . . . something . . . ohhhh! Words fail me. All I know is I do not want to let go of anyone who smells this good.

"Oh, Babylon . . . ?" Izzie's voice singsongs. It seems to come from very far away.

"Babylon?" Another voice. Alden's?

"Hmmm?" I murmur.

"Can you give us your impression?"

I need to snap out of this swoon state; I need to express myself. "This stuff is . . ." Suddenly the words I've been searching for come to me, even though they make no sense. "This stuff . . . it's . . . intoxi-can't-controllable!"

My gobbledygook must hit a target or ring a bell or strike a chord, because I hear a smattering of applause. Then someone lifts my blindfold, and there I am hanging on to Gabe Kandleman, blinking into the depths of his brown eyes and watching his mouth flicker into that infuriatingly semisweet, semi-snarky twist.

"Intoxi-can't-controllable!" says the Sterling-Meadows honcho as I quickly drop my grip on Gabe. "Thank you, Babylon! Thank you very much! I do believe we've got our slogan for Stain!"

Fiery tangerine swirls around pink and purple clouds in the most breathtaking sunset I've ever seen. I'm watching it grow deeper and brighter from the rail as the Kult Kruise yacht heads for the harbor. Oblivious, Paulina, Tabby, and Nae-Jo chat with the Kulterns. Emmalee bowed out of this flirta-a-thon. She's conked out on a deck chair, a shawl draped across her snoozing form. As for me, it's fine to talk shop with the boys of Kult, but I won't put myself in a position that could be construed as disrespectful to Jordan. So I opt for me time, and I've got the spectacular sight all to myself. Or do I?

"Amazing, isn't it?"

I don't have to turn; I know who's there from the faint

trace of Stain wafting toward me. But of course I do turn, just for a second, just to be polite.

"Hey," I say, and quickly look back at the psychedelic sky. "It's incredible, all right."

"It's pollution," Gabe informs me. "Chemtrails. The more particles of dust and ash and soot in the air, the more stunning the sunset. The light bounces in all directions, reflecting off the crap. And New Jersey — that's New Jersey on the other side of the river — Jersey's like the pollution capital of the nation, the armpit of America."

I wonder how much more fairy-tale magic this boy will destroy if I let him keep talking. "Thanks so much," I say. "The chemistry lesson, the geography lesson — illuminating, really."

Gabe seems embarrassed. Well, I guess it's his turn. "Sorry, was I pontificating? I was, wasn't I?" he says. "I do that sometimes. Defense mechanism."

I flick my eyes on him again. "What are you defending yourself against?"

He shrugs. "Look, Babylon, did we get off on the wrong foot or something? Because sometimes my mouth works ahead of my brain, and if I said anything stupid, I want to apologize. We'll be running into each other a lot in the office and, wherever, and I think we should just start over so we can avoid any awkward moments."

As if there could possibly be anything worse than the

way I clung to this boy mere hours ago! Damn that Stain! It ought to be illegal. "Fine," I say, Ms. Eloquence.

At which point we lapse into a silence that would be considered awkward if the changing hues of the wide open sky were slightly less glorious.

THE "WORK IT!" WORKOUT

Sports tone your muscles, but wielding your charm is like exercise for your attitude. Try these smooth moves to get beyond any velvet rope!

Go ahead, you try explaining to your boyfriend that even though it was Saturday, and you were out on a yacht with all these guys — guys that you happened to be *inhaling* — you were hard at work. Jordan left a message for me on Emmalee's voice mail, but once I have a chance to hit him back, I procrastinate. Operation Room Redo is on the agenda for Sunday morning, and it wouldn't be right to make Em do everything. Except I *am* pretty inept at this stuff, so I basically gape while she goes at it. Humming to herself, Emmalee twirls and ties and thumbtacks odds and ends into a sort of baroque bohemian haven. Votive candles add atmosphere, cascades of lace bedeck window and sill, and remarkably, with a few scissor snips, she transforms some colored shopping bags into fabulous paper flowers. When it becomes apparent that I'm only getting in the way, Em nods at her cell with its unlimited free weekend minutes. "Babyl, don't you have a call to make?"

How right she is. It's nearly noon, and soon we'll be leaving for the Unsigned Festival in Tompkins Square — a bunch of bands thus far under my radar. So as my roommate channels Martha Stewart, I seize the empty living room and reach out to my boy.

"Hey you!" Finally! His voice!

"Hey you, yourself!"

"Happy Fourth of July! Oh, Jordan, I miss you so much!" I blurt.

"Me too — I mean, I miss you. So tell me everything!"

Everything? "Well, the girls are awesome — so talented and . . . really interesting. Especially Emmalee — this is her phone; she says hi. Izzie, what can I say, she's brilliant and charismatic . . . yet at the same time so real. It's been crazy; we've been going nonstop. This amazing party . . ." I could name-drop, but I don't. "And then a rally in Central Park, and . . . but what's up there?"

"Huh? Here? Oh, you know, same old same old."

"Like what?" I press for details. "How's work? How's Fiona and Ben?"

"They're cool — joined at the pelvis. Work sucks. Like I said, same old. Oh, except they hired Teri as a cashier."

"Really?" That is big news. The market where Jordan

works always needs summer help. But Teri Quinn? "They must be desperate," I say. "I'd sooner have Britney Spears babysit than trust a Quinn around a cash register!"

"Come on, Babyl — Teri's all right."

That's my Jordan, always seeing the good in people. But I can't believe we're wasting time talking about Teri Quinn! What's next — the weather?

"So is it muggy there?" he asks. "Because here it's been really muggy."

Disbelief — doubled. "No, it's nice. At least yesterday, out on the yacht, with the breeze —"

"The *what*? Did you say *yacht*?"

"Oh, well, I don't know if it really was a *yacht,*" I dismiss it quickly. "It was just this boat, and we were working the whole time."

"Working? Like what — waitressing?"

How to break it down for him? "No, I was . . . it's complicated. Anyway, we're going to the fireworks later — you know, the ones they show on TV every year? Over the Statue of Liberty?"

Pause.

"We're actually going to see them live, down by the river; I'm not exactly sure where. Kult Ink has some hookup — the company is so connected — so we should have a great view."

Silence.

"I wish you could be here to see it with me."

More dead air. Then, "Me too, Babyl," Jordan says at last. "I know it's only been a few days . . . but it feels like . . . I don't know. It feels weird to be without you."

"I know . . ."

Paulina flounces into the living room then, starts mugging and tapping her wrist, like, "Come on." She'd been chewing our ears off all weekend about some act on the Unsigned bill, Red Flamenco or Dead Flamingo or someone. Now Tabby's hustling out of her room, slipping into her backpack, her brand-new, too-tight Sex Pistols T-shirt a misguided stab at punk chic. She's eager to get to Unsigned as well — could be some cute new talent for *Orange*. And here comes Nae-Jo, freshly showered from her ritual morning run, sporting her trademark bikini top and board shorts. The way the three of them ape and clown cracks me up — despite my very important phone call! Emmalee's no doubt ready, too, just doesn't want to rush me.

"Jordan, I need to go," I say.

"Already?" He sounds like a little kid whose ice cream fell in the sand.

"Sorry! I'll call you back, soon as I have a free second."

"Well . . . you better . . ."

Paulina starts stomping and snorting like a robotic bull

with faulty wiring. Where did I leave my bag? My lip balm? My shades?

"Babylon?"

"Yes, of course!" I assure him, and we trade love yous and miss yous and byes. Then Emmalee hooks her arm through mine and we're off.

Since *Squawk* magazine is one of the Unsigned Festival's sponsors, the entire staff ought to be out in force. Everyone must be chilling backstage or in the VIP tent — I don't see a familiar face as we scope out a place to spread our towels. We find a prime location near the stage, but Paulina isn't satisfied. She won't even sit down. Personally I don't care that we didn't get the all-access hookup to the event. It's a *Squawk* thing — along with alterna-station WFMU and sonicsplurge.com, the "downtown download" website — so it has nothing to do with *Orange*. Plus, you can see and hear much better from our spot. Only try and convince Paulina.

"I've *got* to get into that tent," she says. "Tabby, you're the Amuse! Editor of *Orange* magazine. Get over there and squeeze some juice around."

Tabby's already unbuckled her sandals. "Oh, Paulina, they'll want to see passes."

"*Tssss!* Passes! We don't need no stinking passes!" Paulina snaps. "Really, Tabby, if you want to cover entertainment, you better learn how to work it!" She makes an awning of her hand, squints at the entrance. "Well, well, if it isn't Gabe Kandleman manning the entrance."

"Really?" Tabby says. "He's such a cutie."

Only Paulina isn't pointing him out for Tabby's benefit, I'm sure. Last night, she couldn't stop teasing me about the spectacle I made of myself over his Stain-tainted bod. She nudges my leg with the toe of her boot. "Come on, Babyl, let's show these guys how it's done."

I glance around. Nae-Jo's preoccupied by this enormous hero sandwich she's unwrapping — she couldn't care less about the rock show, she just wants to chow down and catch rays. Meanwhile Emmalee, conscientiously reapplying sunscreen, hasn't missed a beat. "You'd best go with her, Babylon," she says. "Paulina's nothing if not single-minded."

No denying that! Plus, I am curious: Will Gabe grant me special privileges, now that we've "started over"? Paulina grabs my wrist and hauls me to my feet.

"I'll be back," I tell Em, who grins enigmatically and pulls down the brim of her huge straw hat.

As we make our way over, Tabby, rebuckled, trots to catch up. "Well!" she says. "I *am* the Amuse! Editor of *Orange,* aren't I? If anyone *deserves* access, it's me!"

Humidity has turned Gabe's curls into a white-boy fro. He must be feeling the heat, because all of a sudden he pulls off his *Squawk* T-shirt and winds it around his head. Do I notice the lean muscles of his back, the hint of boxer shorts poking above his belt, a small, almost indiscernible tattoo on his left shoulder? Of course — it's my journalistic nature to be observant. I'm just deciphering his ink — it's Felix the Cat! — when Tabby burbles: "Woo-hoo! Gabe! Hi, Gabe!"

He turns our way. "Oh, the Run Amoks."

Paulina's too cool for pleasantries, but I say hello. "Nice turban," I add. Actually, he looks kind of silly . . . but somehow he wears silly well.

"Come on, Gabe, let us in!" Ah, Paulina and her subtlety.

"Ahem, I *am* the Amuse! Editor of *Orange*!" Tabby's getting used to this line. "I may want to cover some of these bands in the Run Amok issue." She shifts her weight from hip to hip. "You know what, Gabe? We really need to talk sometime soon. I bet you have the best taste in music. We could go for coffee, and you could tell me who you like . . . musically," she says, hips hyperactivating again.

"Yeah, I guess — whoa, may I?" Gabe turns to check someone's credentials. "Thanks! Enjoy!"

"Come on, dude," Paulina wheedles. "Go tie your shoe so we can sneak in."

That approach will never work — this boy's got ethics. "Gabe, look, they're charging the masses four bucks for a measly pint of water, while the chosen few swill unlimited frosty beverages courtesy of *Squawk*," I reason. "That's not fair."

Gabe makes his face. "So what are you, Babylon, a communist?"

I shrug. "It's a beautiful theory."

"And you want to put it into practice," he says slyly, considering this, then steps away and waves us in.

THE KILLER INSTINCT

Some girls will do anything to get what they want. When the prize is paramount, competition can go from healthy to heinous. How can you tell if you've crossed the line . . . ?

Hello, Monday morning! Nae-Jo is so over the subway — she'll take her board to work. Paulina has barricaded herself in the bathroom, doing who knows what. That leaves Tabby, Emmalee, and me to brave the rush hour train together. Fortunately it's air-conditioned, since we all took pains with our pitch-meeting outfits — I'm even wearing a skirt! — and it would suck if we wilted before we got to the office. Somehow we resist the unprofessional urge to group hug in Kult Ink reception. "Well . . . knock their socks off, you guys," I tell them before we part ways.

"You too, Babylon!" says Tabby.

"But of course you will," adds Emmalee.

Separation anxiety! "So I guess we'll regroup in the meeting . . ."

"The big meeting, yes, at three!" says Emmalee.

"Unless . . . we *are* entitled to a lunch break. Should we meet here at one? We could try that burger place down the block."

Tabby puts her hand up dramatically. "No thank you! I am on a serious diet!" She shows us the can of Slim-Fast in her bag to prove she means it.

That's her prerogative. Me, I hope I can hold out till one. Toothpaste is the closest I got to breakfast. "Great idea, Em — see you then," I say before sallying forth to Natalie's — I mean, *my* — office. Conundrum: The door is closed. Do I knock? Stroll right in? I try the handle but it won't budge. So much for getting a jump start, unless someone else has a key. I retrace my steps to reception.

"Finished for the day?" Finney says.

"Ha-ha." I lean a hand on the desk. "I can't get into my office."

"Wish I could help you, Babylon, but Izzie's assistant's the only one with the master key to all of *Orange*."

Ouch! I'm pretty sure I know who that is — Kult Ink being a stripped-down organization, interns function as assistants around here; college students come cheaper. Resisting the urge to wrinkle my nose, I say, "Matumba?"

"That would be her — only she's not in yet either," Finney says.

Just as I'm musing on my next move, the elevator opens and Natalie falls out, encumbered by purse, canvas tote bag, and ultra-mega-grande iced coffee. The vertical stripes of her button-down shirtdress make her seem even thinner.

"Babylon, forgive me!" Natalie's voice is a soft rasp; her smile wide, natural, and kind of crooked. "Morning, Finney."

"Morning, Nat," he says.

"I had terrible train luck," she explains as we walk down the hall. "Sat in the tunnel for ten inexplicable minutes."

Who can be mad at the subway? "Please, Natalie, no problem! I don't even think you're late — I'm just early." She struggles with her load, trying to locate the key. "Um, can I hold something?" I offer.

Natalie blows a wisp of hair out of her eyes and hands me her half-finished coffee. "Great!" she says when we get inside. "IT already has you set up."

The desk — which is really a table — is in the center of the room, two computers on top. Natalie relieves me of her coffee and sucks it down in three deep sips. "Ah!" she says. "Lifeblood! So, Babylon — are you familiar with Quark?"

The morning flies by as Natalie gives me a nuts-and-bolts tutorial in *Orange* operations — all the phases a story goes through from manuscript to printed page. It's a lot to learn, but fascinating too. "So, when will Izzie read my text?" I ask. "Does she oversee all the stages, or . . ."

Natalie waves some page proofs — these large printouts of text and layout. "Look, Babylon, I don't know what kind of . . . illusions you have . . ." she begins, then changes her tone. "You see, Izzie LaPointe is an extremely busy woman — you can't imagine the demands on her. An E-i-C's role isn't just about concepts, designs, words and pictures, the nitty-gritty of editorial. Izzie has to *be Orange,* and she has to be *Orange* all the time. That's why she has us, a staff she can trust to . . . intuit her vision."

I absorb this. "You mean read her mind?" Seems like a tall order, but I guess if you really *get* the *Orange* ethos — if you understand *Orange,* and by extension Izzie, it ought to come naturally.

"You're a quick study!" Natalie says with her smile askew. "So tell me — have you had a New York slice yet?"

Sounds like some kind of dangerous hazing initiation. "Uh . . . slice?"

"Pizza, Babylon, pizza! There's a great place on Ninth Avenue — thin crust, not too greasy . . . but greasy enough. Any interest?"

Hearing Natalie enthuse over food makes me glad — she's what my mom would call "in need of nourishment." But oops! I completely forgot! I'm supposed to meet Emmalee for lunch. On the other hand I can't just blow off my mentor. The clock on my computer reads a quarter to two — apparently I've already bailed on Em. I push aside the guilt. "Sounds yummy," I say.

The mystery of Paulina's bathroom seclusion is solved the second she struts into the pitch meeting. Her hair, formerly granny smith green, is now neon orange. How industrious, how imaginative, how . . . sneaky. I try to be as chill as Em, and not to let my reaction show. Tabby literally chokes on her water, and Nae-Jo leans in to her, grumbling something I can't hear. As if Paulina cares what we think — she gets the response she wants.

"Your hair is on fire!" Izzie exults when she bustles into the conference room. "Really, Paulina, I love it!"

Paulina beams. "Green was just a phase. Orange always has been my true color."

Izzie takes a seat at the head of the table. "Well, if your design ideas are as inspired as your 'do, the Run Amok issue's going to look great," she says. "So why don't you go first, Paulina?"

Jumping up, Paulina hands everyone color copies of her concepts — and they're fantastic. Even down to the tiniest details, like having a ticker of girls' feet — in sneakers, stilettos, biker boots, ballet shoes, barefoot — along the bottom of every page, to stand for readers running amok. As she talks us through it, Izzie nods along eagerly, completing her sentences with her. Paulina's Create! mentor, Tia Phee, seems totally into it too.

"Great work, Paulina," Izzie lauds, her eyes shining. "It's

so fresh, so twisted! Of course, some of it's prohibitively expensive, but that doesn't matter — what matters is the way you think. Bravo!"

Talk about a tough act to follow — but I don't go next, my girl Emmalee does. I haven't been able to catch her eye since we entered the meeting, and I wonder if she's annoyed that I flaked on lunch. Well, it's not like she came down the hall looking for me either. Whatever, I'll explain later. I throw her an encouraging smile as she stands up to present.

"I'll be brief, since I have both fashion and beauty to pitch," she says. "But I believe I'll be able to convey my beauty concept rather quickly if you'll allow me to bring in my visuals." Emmalee opens the door, and six girls (plus two moms) file in.

"Ladies, if you will . . ." Em says.

"My name is Rebeca Felipe — and I'm beautiful."

"I'm Te'Nana Paige — and I'm beautiful."

"I'm Jessie Franklin — and I'm beautiful."

"I'm Sendra Polanski — and I am beautiful."

"My name is Persis Koli — and I'm beautiful."

Mm-hmm, I'm Babylon Edison, and I'm getting the picture.

"Thank you! Thank you all so much," Emmalee says once the last girl has spoken. "My concept is a celebration of the fact that *every* girl is beautiful. Of course, I have it all written up." She begins to dispense copies of her vision for Stun!

neatly held in transparent folders. "But as I was walking around Chelsea Piers by myself at lunchtime, it occurred to me that all the proudly different but equally beautiful girls I saw could make my point for me."

"And they did!" Izzie pronounces. "Beautifully, I may add. Emmalee, this is genius. 'Every Girl Is Beautiful.' Yes!"

A rosy hue comes to Emmalee's cheeks under Izzie's praise. "Thank you, Izzie," she says. "Of course, I did have to bribe the girls. I told them they could ransack the beauty closet."

What girl wouldn't jump at that chance? The so-called beauty closet is actually an office stocked floor to ceiling with the latest makeup, hair products, bath goodies, nail polish — you name it, a whole shelf dedicated to glitter. Marguerite Aradel, Em's Stun! mentor, laughs indulgently. "My bad, Izzie — I said okay." She turns to the girls. "Angela, our Stun! intern, would be delighted to escort you."

Delighted? Uh — I don't know. The way the overly sun-exposed Angela is scowling in the doorway, I would have used a different word. Angela aims her dagger stare straight at Emmalee, who doesn't acknowledge it in the slightest as her living, breathing proposal clears out, jabbering excitedly. Man, Em sure can be an ice queen when she wants!

"And now," says Emmalee, cool as the proverbial cucumber. "On to fashion!"

I try to concentrate on her "Come As You Are" concept, but my mind wanders. Because A) how she *had* to say she was strolling solo earlier was clearly meant for me and B) the way she seized the lunchtime loner opportunity to kick her pitch to the next level, well, it was smart but also, maybe, a teensy bit cutthroat. Not that Emmalee threatens me in any way. I'm confident in my ability to express myself. Yet I'm feeling a little . . . well, what am I feeling . . . could I actually be jealous of Em?

That's when intellectual lightning strikes. "Girls Helping Girls" — how lame! A much better idea pulls a coup d'etat in my cranium. As Emmalee finishes, and Tabby, then Nae-Jo present, I make notes a mile a minute as thoughts come flying at me. Recent reports I've seen in the papers. Research studies I've noticed online. Observations from the last few days — and the last few minutes! This is not last-minute second-guessing myself; this is pure inspiration. This is thunderbolts and lightning. This is *real*.

When Izzie calls on me, I basically wing it, but unlike the last time I spoke off the cuff to this crowd, I'm not the least bit flustered. I am a verbal machine gun. There is no foiling my flow! Words — the right words, the perfect words — occur to me, a reward for my passion.

Then, when I'm done: Silence. Absolute hear-a-pin-drop silence. I must have blown their minds to Mars. Maybe they weren't expecting me to serve up anything so controversial. Not that it matters what any of them think — except Izzie, of course.

And finally, she says my name. "Babylon . . . oh, Babylon." There's this hint of almost sadness in her voice. "Babylon, Babylon, Babylon. 'The Killer Instinct: How Far Will Girls Go to Get What They Want.' Well, that's certainly a thought-provoking proposal for Think!."

"Girls in our society are on a ruthless rampage," I reiterate. "They'll stop at nothing to tear each other down."

Izzie cocks her head. "Obviously, Babylon, you're extremely articulate, not to mention ardent."

So why am I not hearing the "brilliant!" and "genius!" and similar skyrockets of acclaim Izzie launched at other Run Amoks?

"That's why I'm flabbergasted that you could be so completely off the mark."

"What . . . I'm sorry . . . what do you mean?"

"Babylon, *Orange* rejoices in girls with juice. That is our whole philosophy. We shout girls out, we don't pull them down. We champion young women, we don't trash them. That you would suggest dedicating Think! to such negativity . . ."

Tears begin to well up in my eyes, and Izzie stops talking, pops on her dazzling smile and rises from her seat to rush over to where I still manage to remain standing. She puts her arms around me. "Babylon," she says. "Babylon, Babylon,

Babylon." She gazes into my eyes, strokes my cheek with a finger. "Don't be upset. This is really no biggie. You just went a little astray. But I" — her gaze circulates the room now — "*we* believe in you. We know you can deliver the kind of killer Think! pages girls with juice rely on *Orange* for."

She gives me a squeeze. My hands seem to be frozen into stumps.

I look at Izzie, who's still hugging me. And somehow I cough out: "I do . . . I do have another idea. It's really positive, and —"

"Great, Babylon!" she says, and gives me one final squeeze before striding back to her side of the table. "And I really want to hear it." She collects her BlackBerry and notepad and platinum-trimmed fountain pen. "E-mail me a memo and I'll look at it first thing." Those bright eyes and smile survey the room once more. "Great stuff, you guys, all of you! I'm so impressed!"

Izzie reaches for the door, then swivels on her kitten heels. "Oh, Paulina — I almost forgot. There's an opening at the Mailer Gallery tonight — this remarkable collagist, her name escapes me at the moment. Anyway, Carlo hates those kinds of things. . . ."

That's Carlo Barbosa, Brazilian soccer star, the suitor Izzie's seen most about town with these days, according to the tabloids.

"You want to be my plus one?"

DO YOU HAVE BOUNCE-BACK ABILITY?

When *sucky stuff happens*, do you curl up in a ball and pull the covers over your head? Or shake it off and come out swinging?

Good thing *Orange* doesn't have an "embarrassing moments" page, or I'd be a prime candidate. The mortification of the pitch meeting will no doubt haunt me forever, far more than any period-in-white-pants story ever could. Of course, Izzie was great about the whole thing. But how could I have been so wrong, wrong, wrong?

"Babylon?" Natalie approaches as I sit in our office, attempting to collect myself. "I'm going to the deli — you want anything? A soda? Frozen yogurt?"

As if empty calories could improve my mood! "No thank you, Natalie," I say, my voice still thin and shaky, a stranger's voice.

"Look, if it's any consolation, what happened . . . well, it happens to every journalist," she says gently, leaning against the desk. "I've been shot down millions of times . . . and . . . you have to develop a thick skin in this business.

Rejection sucks, but you know the old adage: Whatever doesn't kill you makes you stranger."

What? I look up at her crossways; she almost smiles. "And stronger," she says.

At least she acknowledges the depths of my devastation. It would be worse if she were to play it off like nothing. "I appreciate that," I say, steeling myself to put the miserable mess behind me. "Guess I need to e-mail Izzie my other pitch."

Natalie smiles for real. "That's the spirit!" she says. "You're sure you don't want a snack though? I think you underestimate the curative powers of fro-yo."

I shake my head and she doesn't push it, just leaves me to deal. And that's what I do: write and rewrite a memo, attach "Girls Helping Girls," and press SEND. The second I do, an IM pops up from Emmalee:

e.roberts: it's nearly 6. are you about ready to leave?
b.edison: #@%$* yeah!
e.roberts: general tso's tofu? moo-shu shrimp?
b.edison: u r reading my mind.

It's the idea of hanging with Emmalee, not General Tso, that comforts me. I'm still not hungry, but if Em was mad about lunch, she's moved past it, and knowing that actually makes me feel a little better. Half a second later my computer dings again.

e.roberts: so . . . n-j & t?

I don't want to snub my fellow Run Amoks. And I'll have to face them sooner or later. But I opt for later.

b.edison: v. exclusive party 2nite. just u/me.

Boy Attention Deficit Disorder, or BADD, has afflicted Paulina big-time. The film student she met her first night in town has been kicked to the curb in favor of Rek, her latest conquest, whom she met at the gallery opening with Izzie. She's been blathering on about him for three days straight now. Here's a sample: "His real name is Marek, he's Czech — Rek the Czech! His dad's some kind of diplomat. Damn, is he hot — looks like Gerard from My Chemical Romance. And he rides a Vespa . . ."

Blah-blah-blah. Tuning her out, I wonder how Paulina expects to accomplish anything this summer, what with all her extracurriculars. Rampant boy-hopping doesn't really go with the *Orange* ethos either. Personally, I aim to fully embrace *Orange* as a lifestyle, including the emphasis on health and fitness, so I've started running along the river each morning with Nae-Jo. Of course, "with" is a misnomer — she basically leaves me in the dust — but it's nice to be out early, filling my lungs with smog, watching the tugboats chug along. I feel a certain affinity with tugboats; they're not glamorous but they get the job done. Today, Tabby decides to join us — part of her weight-loss plan, I presume. Again, her business, but a girl with juice should be comfortable in her own skin.

Comfortable in her own mind too — but I had a porcupine nesting in my cranium waiting for Izzie to weigh in on "Girls Helping Girls." Finally she granted clearance yesterday, via e-mail, no message, just "go for it" in the subject bar. That's exactly what I'm doing, immersing myself in research, scouring the Internet for girls who were there for each other during natural disasters, bouts of illness and addiction, homelessness, all kinds of terrible circumstances. I'm into it, I really am. Yet when Tabby interrupts me this afternoon, I manage to drag myself away.

"Ooh, Babylon, guess what? You'll never guess! Turpentine Cocktail are going to be in the Run Amok issue! Isn't that amazing?"

The way the girl hops around, you'd think someone installed a Dance Dance Revolution machine in my office. "Killer, Tabby," I say. Although it does strike me as weird. The concept Izzie endorsed for Amuse! was "Next Big Knockouts" — basically unknowns that *Orange* predicts will be huge in the coming year. But Turpentine Cocktail are already bona fide emo heroes. Plus, they've already been featured in *Orange*. "Only how do we rationalize TC as up-and-comers?" I feel compelled to point this out.

"Actually, it was Izzie's idea," Tabby explains. "You see, *we're* up on TC because *we're* girls with juice. But *Orange* is gaining new readers all the time, so girls who are just getting into the magazine have to be tipped off to bands like TC. If we don't do that, we're not serving our audience."

Izzie's so smart about stuff like that — she really sees the big picture. "Okay, makes sense," I tell Tabby. "Still, it will take some clever writing skills to introduce the band to new readers without offending longtime loyalists." Fiona comes to mind — she's a big TC fan, and I can practically hear her scoff: "Turpentine Cocktail? *Next?* In what solar system?" Not that she wouldn't be psyched to read an interview and see some new photos.

"Well, that's what I came to talk to you about," Tabby says. "I was thinking about the interview, and naturally I'm dying to do it myself — but I'm going to be so busy coordinating. Then I was like: Babylon! She could really use a perk, and what better pick-me-up than getting up close and personal with Turpentine Cocktail!"

Mm-hmm, I see: Tabby wants to hang with the band but would rather not transcribe a lengthy interview or conceive an intelligent approach to the piece — so she's considerate enough to offer those crumbs to me. However, I do dig TC.

The music's a bit mopey, but sometimes I'm in the mood for that, and they're cool, with their coed, multiethnic lineup and their insistence on keeping ticket prices real.

"Tabby, you're sweet to think of me," I tell her. "But I'm swamped too."

She stares at me as though I sneezed in her Slim-Fast. "You — Babylon — you're not thinking of turning this down?"

Actually, no, I'm not. But Tabby has to understand that I'm the one doing her a favor, not vice versa. "I'd hate to, but . . . when's this all supposed to go down?"

"Friday at five, at the Hammerstein Ballroom, after sound check," she says.

"Ooh, see, that's no good," I shake my head. "I've got other plans . . . but if you really need me, I guess I could reschedule. . . ."

"Oh, Babylon, could you?" Tabby begs.

I sigh. "I will get a byline on the story, right?" One can never assume.

"Of course!" she says. "Turpentine Cocktail by Babylon Edison!"

Has a nice ring to it.

EXCLUSIVE EXPOSURE!
SHOCKING SECRETS!
CRAZY CONFESSIONS!

Gossip is tawdry, trifling, and just plain silly. Not to mention fascinating, delicious, and simply irresistible. And if you think rock star revelations are juicy, wait till you hear what some of your closest friends will dare admit!

Watching a sound check is like having a semiprivate mini-concert. Mini, because the band doesn't rehearse the entire set; the purpose is just to test the equipment of the venue. And semi, since the Hammerstein Ballroom isn't exactly empty. Tabby is here, "coordinating," along with Berni, her Amuse! mentor. Record company people, Hammerstein people. Members of TC's road crew and entourage.

Everyone's pretty nice, which keeps my nerves in check. I've never interviewed a band before, but I'm prepared. I know their albums backward and forward, and I've figured out my angle: The Amuse! section can open on Turpentine

Cocktail, and instead of a straight profile, I'll structure the piece around their picks for the next big knockouts.

Berni introduces me to Rachel, TC's publicist, a giraffe-necked woman with eighties hair (which I doubt is meant to be ironic; she just hasn't updated her 'do since Cyndi Lauper was hot), who shepherds me backstage into a surprisingly no-frills room. There — whoa! — I come face-to-face with Mute Ahidjo, TC's fine-physiqued, chisel-faced, African-born, Midwest-raised front man. The sensitive sex god behind "Abuse in A Minor" and "The Slap" is a foot away, smiling at me. Fiona would die! The rest of the band lounge on a ratty sofa.

"Guys, this is Babylon from *Orange*," Rachel says.

"'Come we go chant down Babylon,'" Mute sings a line from the reggae tune I've known since the cradle in his deep, mellifluous voice. "So your parents are into Bob Marley?" He smiles wider — his teeth even more perfect in person than on MTV.

"Wow," I say, melting in place. "It's so nice not to have to explain. All my life it's been, 'what kind of name is *that*?'"

He laughs, showing more remarkable teeth — even his molars rock! "Don't I know it, growing up in Des Moines with a moniker like Muteso!"

Way to break the ice! I breathe easy as I click on my tape recorder. Turpentine Cocktail treat me like a regular person, and they're regular people too — except, you know, with talent and fame. Only trouble is, drummer Julian's being snotty — literally. He has a nasty cold, and it must be affecting his brain, because he takes a sip from bassist Nadja's cup. Mistake!

"Goddamn it, Julian — that's so passive-aggressive!" Nadja cries. "Do you *want* me to get sick? Just because I've banned your germy contagious tongue from my throat!"

Uhh . . . what? I wonder.

"Nadja!" thunders Mute, who looks at her and then at me and then back at her with ire in his eyes.

"Oh . . ." Nadja eats her knuckles. "Oh, shit."

Everyone's quiet for a few seconds, then Julian blows his nose noisily. I look at him, then at Nadja. They look busted. They look guilty. They look in love! And everyone knows I know!

"Look, Babylon, we have a policy to not discuss our personal relationships with the press," Mute recites. "It just isn't relevant . . . it distracts from the music."

With plenty of questions left, I don't want the band to clam up, bring the interview to a hasty close. Better tread lightly. "I can understand that," I say carefully, yet noncommittally. "Now, Lili, you mentioned a band you met while on tour in Argentina. Do you know if they'll have a record out in the States?"

Somehow I succeed in moving them past Nadja's faux

pas, but my mind is wheeling, reeling, and dealing. Turpentine Cocktail's Nadja and Julian — a couple! This is some scoop! Now I just have to decide what to do with it.

"Emmalee, can I tell you something?" Tell? More like scream. It's between bands at the Hammerstein, the crowd so loud I still have to yell.

"Of course, Babyl — what is it?"

I grab her hand and we weave through the throng for a quieter spot. Being out with Em is a trip — the way guys stare and girls snarl, and her not seeming to care about either. "It's a matter of ethics, and I don't know what to do," I say when we secure a nook. "But it's a secret too. A big one."

She tosses her hair, worn in shimmering loose waves tonight. "Babylon, are you asking if you can trust me?"

Maybe I am. Usually I consider myself an excellent judge of character, and Em's been nothing but a real friend so far. Only the stakes seem so much higher in this city; I feel like I need to read between every line, question every smile. It's getting to the point where I don't know if I trust myself. "Because you *can,*" she says.

I really need advice, so I lay out what I learned in the TC interview. "Bottom line, this is news, and if my allegiance is to *Orange* I wouldn't think twice about exposing Nadja and Julian. I don't *owe* Turpentine Cocktail my silence. But the angle of my story has nothing to do with who's swapping spit with who. So what do I do? Tell Tabby and let her make the call? Bring it to Izzie's attention? Ugh!"

Emmalee leans against the wall. "This *is* a quandary," she says.

Just then she drops her eyes — and one glance over my shoulder tells me she hasn't become abruptly bored with my conundrum. Two guys encroach, wearing that look boys get when Emmalee's around. They're beyond smitten; it's like they want to bite her or something. "Hey," they say. I flip my hip while Emmalee examines the floor tiles. This is her deal, but since she does nothing — except maybe pray for a trapdoor to open beneath her wedges — I throw tact to the wind. "There are three things you guys should know straight up," I snap. "We *don't* want a drink, we *don't* know the time, and we have no *idea* when Turpentine Cocktail go on. Any *other* questions?"

The way they back off, tripping over each other, it's like a cartoon. Even when one of them sneers the *B* word at me, he comes off so flustered it's comical. Instantly Emmalee raises her eyes and picks up where we left off. "All I can suggest is that you live with the information for a while," she continues. "Sometimes you have to wait for answers to reveal themselves to you."

"Nice try, O Wise One, but you're not getting off that

easy," I say. Behind the regally regained composure, Emmalee's still rattled, her breathing shallow and her spine stiff. "Will you please explain to me what just went down here?"

"Pardon me?" she says formally. But she knows. And she knows I know she knows.

Still, I'll spell it out. "With your endless stream of male attention, you ought to be a pro at telling guys off by now. Let alone flirting back if they're worthy."

Emmalee purses her lips and lets her gaze flit around before coming to rest on mine. "Do you really want to know?" she asks. "Because I *could* tell you, Babylon —"

I nod. "Trust is a two-way street."

Emmalee sighs. "All right . . . so perhaps you've noticed — me . . . and boys . . . the twain do not meet," she says. "Which is insane. Babylon, I am utterly and completely into boys. On paper. In theory. But when a flesh-and-blood boy looks at me, I freeze. I'm scared. Of what? I don't know!"

Her words really rush and tumble now, an avalanche of verbiage: "I don't know why either. It's not like my parents are overprotective or hugely religious or any such thing. In fact, my mother wrings her hands over what could be wrong with me. And there is something wrong, there must be. Everybody — here, back home — thinks I'm stuck up or some kind of super-prude. And I'm not. But I am! You could fit my sexual experience on the head of a pin and still have room for a picnic. I've never been on a date or ridden alone with a boy in a car or . . . Babylon, I'm seventeen years old, and I've never even been kissed!"

Just when you thought you'd heard it all, *wham!* A meteor. Of course, Emmalee's confession explains a lot — the way she blew off Duncan Branch at Club Cargo, her seeming snootiness around the Kulterns. "Well, I'm glad you told me," I say.

"What? That I'm a freak?" Unburdened, she can almost laugh.

"You're not a freak, you're . . . what's it called? A late bloomer," I say. "Look, not every girl has Paulina's hormones — if you want to talk about freaks. . . ."

"Babylon!" Em shrieks daintily behind her fingertips. "She is, isn't she?"

"Is she trying to set a record or something? I think Rek the Czech's already been bounced."

"Incredible!"

We trade smiles. "So we still have time to kill before Turpentine Cocktail goes on. You want to do the backstage thing?" Tabby got all the Run Amoks passes from the publicist.

"We might as well," Em says. "We do have a reputation for fabulousness to maintain."

It's actually pretty fun. TC must be holed up in their dressing room, but Mansions of Happiness, the opening band, is holding court and clowning around. The predictable cast of hangers-on, fledgling models, record label people are here. Naturally, the New York music media is in full effect. Its members are easy to spot — mostly male, working that nerd-chic thing while downing courtesy Heinekens and checking out the Mischa Barton clones. Funny, two weeks ago this world was totally foreign to me. Now spending Friday night like this feels almost normal.

Tabby is carrying on like a runaway train in a fresh manicure and trendy gear — she might not have had time to do the interview but she found a few minutes to get her nails done and plow through Urban Outfitters. Still, you have to admire her schmooze skills. Nae-Jo and Paulina are chatting up some guys, but Em and I opt to hang back and observe. That's when TC's Nadja and Lili come over to talk with us. I figure Emmalee knows who they are, but I make introductions all around.

Lili touches the edge of Emmalee's tulip sleeve. "I love your shirt. Is it vintage?"

"Vintage Goodwill," Em says. "It used to be a dress, but the bottom was hideous."

While Em and Lili trade thrift shop scores, Nadja says to me: "Sorry if I was a bitch earlier, or a brat or whatever."

Is she trying to butter me up, so I won't expose her secret? "Please, no problem!" I toss it off, then steer the convo away. "You and Lili seem so relaxed. You never get stage fright?"

"Not anymore," she says. "I used to be a basket case before gigs, but we've been doing this so long. Now I just can't wait to get out and rock."

"Uh-oh!" Lili nudges Nadja. "Check it out, Nadj — Noel's on the prowl again."

Nadja tsks. "Noel's our manager," she explains. "He's pushing fifty, divorced twice, but still a total player. Come on, Lil, let's go give him shit."

As they go off, I follow with my eyes — and see that his girl de nuit is none other than Izzie LaPointe!

Emmalee's noticed too. "They sure look cozy," she says, "ew" implied. "I thought Izzie was into that soccer player."

The two have their arms draped around each other, Noel with his thumb stuck in the belt loop of Izzie's jeans. "I don't think that's exclusive," I say quickly in Izzie's defense. "Besides, Izzie and that Noel guy could just be platonic. I'm sure it's common for editors and managers to fraternize."

"Oh, I'm sure that happens all the time," Em agrees. "In fact, that's probably why TC is going in the Run Amok issue."

I'm about to explain Izzie's rationale for including the band, as Tabby explained it to me, when Gabe comes up.

"Hey, Babylon, heard you interviewed Turpentine Cocktail today!"

"Oh, hey, Gabe." No shock that he's here, he's such a music hound. I bet he'll be E-i-C of *Squawk* one day. "You remember Emmalee."

"Sure, hey, Emmalee," he says.

She gives him a small smile and a hi — I guess she feels safe around guys who don't look at her "that way." And Gabe isn't looking at her at all. He's looking at me.

"So what were they like — TC, I mean? Man, I'm impressed. The only things I've gotten to write for *Squawk* so far is captions, and I've been their slave boy since March. Oh, and one obit — can't forget that. You get to write about live rock stars, Babylon, I only get to write about dead ones!"

"Hey! Gabe! Oh, Jesus, I'm going to have a heart attack!" Finney rushes up, huffing and puffing, and grabs Gabe's sleeve. "Dude! Guess who's here? Chris Martin from Coldplay! Don't look! Okay, now — look! It's him, isn't it?"

Finney's so psyched, Em and I don't even register in his consciousness, but I forgive him, since when I look in that direction I get a little light-headed to see Mrs. Martin, aka Gwyneth Paltrow.

"That's him, right?!" Finney blathers. "Right? Come on, Gabe, let's go talk to him. Or not, you know, *talk* — but just, you know, get close enough *to* talk if it was feasible for us to not say anything stupid."

Off they go, and Emmalee grins at me — a grin she's trying not to grin but cannot help grinning. "As we both know, I'm no authority on boys," she says. "But that one is so into you!"

My cheeks warm slightly at the comment. But before I can counter with a "don't be silly" or a "we're just friends," or remind her that I'm with Jordan, Tabby descends on us. "Babylon! Emmalee!" she hollers, zooming in for air kisses. "Isn't this the best night? I am having the best time! Aren't Mansions of Happiness awesome? We should definitely put them in the issue! I have to tell you, Babyl, I saw you talking to Gabe just now, oh, I was talking with him for like an hour before. He is so nice. And so smart! He knows everything about music."

What is she, his publicist now? Why is everyone gabbing about Gabe, Gabe, Gabe?!

"And cute!" she blathers on. "And best of all, he's Jewish! Oh, I have such a crush on him!"

What? Tabby and Gabe? Why does this confession hit me like a dodgeball made of lead?

"Babyl, I know you're friends with him," Tabby says. "So do me a favor? Talk to him about me — find out if he likes me? Pleeeeeze?"

MODEL MATERIAL

What happens when a pretty girl is suddenly thrust into the dizzying, dazzling world of professional posing? Well, first she has to contend with her so-called friends....

Magazine editors live in a time warp. Here it is, July 21, but we're immersed in winter, putting together a December issue when the rest of the hemisphere is all about Frisbees, barbecues, and tan lines. It's got to be weirdest for Emmalee: One of her fashion shoots is a collection of winter gear, so she's up to her eyeballs in parkas, sweaters, and boots. Just mouthing the word "wool" right now makes me sweat. Fortunately her "Come As You Are" concept is for holiday fashion, and nobody wears bulky stuff to party. Even better, she got permits to shoot at Coney Island, so just when cold weather really hits, *Orange* readers can feel like they're at the beach.

"Hey, Babylon? Can you scout with me in Union Square after work? Please?" Em pops into my office, sweetly beseeching.

The winter gear shoot is a "still life," aka clothes without people in them, but Em needs real girls to appear in both "Come . . ." and "Every Girl Is Beautiful." I've gone casting with her twice already, chatting up more chicks than the Sprouse twins at a *Zack and Cody* meet-and-greet. "Do I have to?" I ask.

"Yes," she says, "because Paulina insists on coming, and while I'm pleased to see her apply herself to something other than the nearest male, she and I . . . well, we don't always see eye to eye on who would make a good *Orange* model. I need you around . . . to be impartial."

True enough, but I bet that's not all there is to it. The dynamic between those two has been tense the last few days, Paulina cracking on some of the "cutsie-wootsie" and "puk-ily preppy" styles Em selected for the still life. Much as I respect Paulina's taste — and as Create! Editor, she does get to weigh in on all visuals — she could be more diplomatic about the way she expresses herself. It's got to rankle Emmalee, who'd never be anything less than ladylike.

"Okay, I'll go — if you'll help me wade through all these 'Girls Helping Girls' girls." I flail a stack of printouts, without mentioning I'm a bit behind because I was on the phone all morning with Jordan. He had the morning off, so we were finalizing the details of his NYC trip — hurry up, August 1 — and just generally cooing at each other, Natalie being nice enough to give me the office to myself. I'm so looking forward to reconnecting in person, and I've inked the date of his arrival in my mind. But now it's time to get back to business. "I need to narrow the field to fifteen," I tell Em, "so tomorrow Nat and I can pick six finalists for Izzie."

Natalie peeks up from her computer. "That's right," she says. "Deadlines wait for no woman!"

Emmalee takes a seat and together we pore over the pages — until we are rudely interrupted.

"So this is where you've been hiding out!" Matumba stands at the door, hands on her hips. "Honestly, I'm going to have to put leashes on you *editors,*" she says irritably. "Emmalee, no one in Stun! has any idea where you went, Marguerite is in a panic, and I e-mailed you twenty minutes ago! Izzie wants to see you, and she's already late for an appointment in midtown, and —"

"Ah, here you are, Emmalee. Helping out Babylon, I see." Izzie bustles into the office, enormous black sunglasses shielding half her face in preparation to hit the street. "Listen, one of the girls we chose for our November Stun! shoot came down with chicken pox, so I need you to jump in and save the day."

Emmalee snaps to like a soldier being called to duty. "Of course, Izzie," she says. "My castings aren't complete yet, but I've got a bunch of Polaroids of cute girls. Should I just run and get them?"

Izzie fixes Emmalee with one of her special Izzie smiles. "Oh, Emmalee — that's why I love you! You're so humble, so modest."

Emmalee blinks rapidly, as if to decode what our editor-in-chief is getting at.

"Emmalee, Emmalee, Emmalee — it's *you* I want in the shoot. That hair, those eyes — this juice!" She gives Emmalee a little squeeze on the shoulder. "How exciting is that?! You get to edit one issue, and model in another. Plus, you'll be helping me out, big-time. And that's what it's all about, right, Babylon? Girls helping girls? So go see Marguerite about the specifics, Emmalee, *stat!*"

All the Run Amoks pitch in with Emmalee's scouting mission in Union Square. Tabby snagged us passes to an anime festival that starts in an hour, so the plan is to divide and conquer, armed with Polaroid cameras and Marguerite's *Orange* business cards to prove that we're legit. When we regroup in front of the theater, Emmalee spills about her upcoming gig.

"Can you imagine?" she moans. "The last thing I want to do is model!"

This damsel's distress is not exactly met with support.

"Why?" asks Tabby, doling out tickets. "If the girl who got chicken pox was zaftig and sultry instead of some pale, puny thing, I'd volunteer in a heartbeat."

"Yeah, really!" says Nae-Jo. "Why hide behind the scenes? Give front and center a try for once."

Em cups her elbows. "It's different for you, Nae-Jo," she says. "You're an athlete, and when the cameras are all over you, it'll be for something you *do* — your abilities, your achievements — not how you *look*."

I want to have Emmalee's back on this, I do. But it's hard to believe any girl would bitch about having her picture in *Orange*.

"Poor little pretty girl!" Paulina rolls her eyes. "I feel so sorry for you, posing with all those hot guys."

Huh? "What hot guys?" I want to know.

"*Create!* can't stop buzzing about this shoot," she says. " 'Beauty and the Brawn,' it's called. The models will pose with the country's top male athletes — football, basketball, wrestling, swimming, lacrosse. Oh, the agony!"

It doesn't sound very *Orange* to me, but I'm sure Izzie has some rationale for it — boys as the backdrop, girls in the limelight, something like that.

"Don't worry, Em — they won't give you cooties," taunts Nae-Jo.

Tabby mimics Emmalee perfectly: "Ick! Insect repellent!"

Snickers all around. I can't help it — I laugh too. Emmalee burns with indignation as she flounces down the theater aisle, takes a seat, crosses her legs, and stares at the blank screen. I file in and sit down next to her, but I don't say a thing. What *can* I say? I feel sort of guilty for joining the giggle gaggle — the last thing I want to do is make fun of Em for being guy-shy. But her complaints about modeling just don't ring true. After all, if she dreads appearing in the shoot so bad, why didn't she dip into her vast supply of courteous charm and simply tell Izzie no thank you?

ARE YOU UTTERLY AND COMPLETELY BLAH?

If it seems as though every other girl has got it going on, and you're just a shade shy of invisible, maybe you need to see yourself through someone else's eyes.

Allow me to introduce myself. I'm Babylon Edison, aka nobody. Look at me! I am, in the dressing-table mirror, and all I see is blah. Because this is New York City — one big bowl of ethnic Chex Mix. I'm not the standout here I was in Southie. I'm ordinary! Average! Average height, average weight, medium complexion, nothing striking, nothing special, a jeans and T-shirts nobody. To make an impression here, you've got to have in-your-face style or some truly imposing physical asset. Yeah, I know what I said about coming here to learn, but that doesn't mean I want to be invisible. So I've pulled out my Bantu knots (which were beyond busted), washed my hair (which is currently congealing into a nondescript mess), and am staring at the irrefutable facts. I'm insipid! Inconspicuous! Goddamn dull!

Especially compared to my suite mates. Bustily bodacious

Tabby. Nae-Jo of the rock-hard limbs. Tall, fierce, flame-haired Paulina. And lest we forget the flawless porcelain statuette that is Emmalee, who bit the bullet and had her big modeling debut today. I am so not in the mood for her when she waltzes into our room to collapse on her bed. She lies there, lashes at half-mast, without a word.

"So?" Suddenly mortified to be caught staring at my mundane self, I turn from the mirror and address Emmalee's comatose form. "Aren't you going to tell me about your miserable day?"

At first, all she says is "oh," or maybe it's "no." It's so breathy I'm not sure. Then she says, "Miserable? Oh. No. Not. At. All."

It sounds like she's speaking from the third ring of Saturn. Is the girl on drugs? Her face is impassive except for the slightest hint of smile, her skin glows more than usual — must be some special moisturizer from the shoot. Her arms lay limp at her sides and her misty gaze fixes on the ceiling.

"So . . . what are you up to?" she asks, preempting my what-the-hell-is-wrong-with-you? strike.

"Me?" I say. "Oh, I'm just sitting here contemplating a waist-length weave and a few facial piercings."

"Really?" she responds from the stratosphere. "Wow . . ."

Okay, now I'm getting concerned. "Emmalee? Are you feeling all right?" I ask. "Or did you stop off for a helium transfusion on your way back to the dorm?"

A silver-bell jingle of laughter from the bed. "No, Babylon," she says. "Just so tired . . . so drained . . ."

Well, she did have a six A.M. call time. Plus, I've heard it's illegal for models to actually eat.

Then she says, "And . . ."

"And what?" She's really starting to worry me!

"And . . . I met someone. . . ."

"Whoa. Wait. What?! You met — you mean . . . as in . . . ?"

"Yes!" Emmalee's ecstasy wafts toward me. "Babylon, I met a boy!"

I fly over to her bed. "Are you kidding? Emmalee, tell me everything!"

His name is John. Simple. Classic. John. John Henry Maxwell. He plays lacrosse for Beddington Corners High School in Beddington Corners, West Virginia. He intends to become a lawyer. Possibly run for Congress. But not before the Peace Corps. He is sweet, sensitive, and strapping (strapping?!), with soulful brown eyes. Emmalee describes him as she deftly trims and shapes my hair, then anoints it with a remarkably effective combination of all the tress-taming products to be found in a bathroom shared by five girls. She's still describing him when she's done with my 'do, but takes a breather to admire her handiwork.

"Yes, mm-hmm, I like it," she says. "What do you think?"

I take a look. Loose, natural, with three inches of zigzag

117

part. Maybe the new 'do won't make jaws drop all over Manhattan, but it's damn cute! I can't wait for Jordan to see it.

"You're amazing!" I give Emmalee a hug. "So? What's next for you and John Henry Maxwell?"

What she tells me almost breaks my heart in half. John Henry Maxwell is already on a plane back to Beddington Corners. A yelp of protest spews from me spontaneously, but Emmalee presses her index finger to her lips.

"No, Babylon, hush," she says. "It's perfect this way. We met — and we knew. We were surrounded by all these people — yet it was just us two. We were working — except we were in paradise. I had to pose with his arms around me for hours, and I have never felt so safe or sublime in my life. We *will* meet again, I know it — and when we do, it will be as though we'd never been apart. And that's when we'll kiss."

Okay, I feel like I stumbled into the script of a G-rated chick-flick fairy tale, but I smack down the sarcasm. "Oh, Emmalee! I'm so happy for you!"

"Well, you should be," she says. "After all, if it wasn't for you, John and I . . . goodness, there probably would be no John and I."

Of course, here in the real world, there really is no John and her, but whatever. "What do you mean, Em? I wasn't even there," I say.

"But you were there the other night, when you let me

tell you my secret. Don't you see? Voicing it aloud, hearing you say it was okay, that . . . released me. Broke the spell. You made this all possible."

"Oh. Well," I say, "that's what friends are for."

"What's what friends are for?" asks Nae-Jo, passing our room.

Em and I smile at each other. Trust. That's what friends are for. "Haircuts," I say, turning to Nae. "Friends are for haircuts — excellent haircuts."

"Whoa, Babyl, you look gooood!" she says. "Emmalee, you did that? Do me! Come on, chica, what do you think — bangs, maybe?" She comes in, cops a squat, and slips off the button-down topping her wifebeater. And that's when we see it. Right there on her left bicep — the *Orange* logo inked onto her flesh!

Three down, three to go. My new 'do must have cleared some brain fuzz, since three days later I've finished half my interviews for "Girls Helping Girls." There's Sydney, who rescued a stranger from a burning car after an accident; Lianne, who trained a seeing-eye dog for her best friend who went blind; and Sara, a Special Olympics coach. Incredible, inspiring girls — so kind, so generous, so selfless. So how come I'm not gung-ho about writing their profiles? Nae-Jo's new ink may have something to do with it.

"Pretty smart, huh?" We're at the fitness station by the

running path, and how she can brag while executing chin-ups is beyond me. "Paulina practically choked when I showed her. And Izzie — well, you saw her reaction."

Indeed I did. It was at Check-In, the weekly meeting where we discuss the progress of our stories, and Nae-Jo wasn't about to wait for our E-i-C to notice. She strutted on up and flexed in Izzie's face before the forum began. Izzie was so blown away she had us cool our heels for ten minutes while the two of them trotted over to the Kult Ink CEO's corner office to show Alden Beck the permanent testament to Nae-Jo's juice.

"You did it to win points with Izzie?" That's right — I just ask her straight up. So far, we've all managed to skirt the issue of the column contest, the big purple elephant in the room that no one will talk about. But clearly it's been on my mind, and I know I'm not the only one. Here, out by the river, away from all things *Orange,* seems a good place to broach the topic.

"What, you think I'm about to let Paulina play me with that hair-dye maneuver?" Nae-Jo's on the hand-over-hand ladder now, swinging herself with simian ease from one rung to the next. "Look, Babylon, that column is going to be mine, and it's not that I *need* the tat to get it. The Move! section is turning out fantastic; I've got skaters, snowboarders, the most extreme chicks ever giving me their secret tips. So I'm good." She gets into position for sit-ups, grinning at me. "*Orange* on my arm just shows my dedication. It's the icing on the cake."

That icing sticks in my brain like a pesky tune. So rather than focus on "Girls Helping Girls" when I get into work, I find myself surfing the Net — randomly, or so it feels at first. But I'm clicking on stuff about female rivalry gone haywire.

"Babylon?" Natalie brings me back to the matter at hand. "We ought to head down to Create!"

I save my file as "Girls vs. Girls" and hustle down the hall to discuss art and photo ideas for my stories. After all, I've got plenty — the quiz, the health Q&A and real-life advice columns, the Girls on the Street Survey (it's about spirituality this month, ideal for the holiday season), and the oh-so-important Tang! page are all part of Think!. We get those pieces out of the way before moving on to my main feature. My concept for "Girls Helping Girls" is simple: just supply the subjects with digital cameras and have them take pictures of themselves, their world, and the people whose lives they've impacted. Then Paulina could do some sort of collage with the images. I think it would look cool, yet talking about it almost feels like faking.

After the meeting, I crank like mad. Coffee is fuel for concentration, and by late afternoon I'm satisfied enough to deliver my drafts to Natalie for editing.

"These look good," she says. "You definitely have command of the language, Babylon. You're a good reporter too. . . ."

I sense a "but" tingeing the compliment. "Thanks," I say. "But?"

"Well, you need to smooth out a few clunky transitions, and you've got a run-on sentence here as long as a large intestine."

"Okay," I say, feeling that there's still something bothering her. "And . . . ?"

"Look, Babylon, this has nothing to do with your skills, but these profiles, they're virtually the same thing that we do in Tang!"

Now that she mentions it, I see she's right. Tang! rhapsodizes girls with juice, and so do the three stories I just wrote. But there's one big difference. "I hear you, Natalie, except Tang! girls are nominated by their friends."

Natalie gives a quick little grunt. "Yeah, right," she mutters.

"They're not?" I ask.

Her expression is inscrutable. "Sorry — of course, they are," she says. Then her inherent honesty takes over. "Usually."

It's as though Natalie wants to tell me something, but I have to ask the right questions to decode the disclosure. "If their friends don't nominate them, who does?"

Natalie taps her pen against the desk. "Not me," she says.

Somehow I know the answer. "Izzie?"

"Well, Tang! is one of her favorite pages," Natalie allows. "And Izzie knows so many people. Powerful, influential people . . ." she trails off.

I fill in the blanks. Some of those powerful, influential people must have teenage daughters or nieces. So Tang! basically functions as a repository for Izzie's important associates. Natalie watches the thoughts take shape in my mind until she can read them on my face. This funny laugh — regretful and relieved and resigned — comes out of her. "Look, Babylon — we're not making Hebrew National frankfurters here," she says finally. "You might as well know there are aspects to the fourth estate that aren't strictly kosher."

Then she begins to scribble rapidly. "Anyway, these pieces are solid," she says without looking up. "All you have to do is tweak the format, so they have a different feel from Tang! Just insert some subheads to break up the text. Like this, see?"

I do see. I see that Natalie has given me a crucial lesson — one that has nothing to do with inserting subheads. But I take the pages back from her and make my tweaks, pausing only to wish her good night when she calls it a day. And when Emmalee e-mails me for my ETD, I tell her to take off without me. I need to stick around and tackle the Turpentine Cocktail piece. It's nearly nine by the time I feel like I've got the story outlined (the Julian–Nadja liaison omitted — it just didn't feel right). My eyes must be saucer-sized with strain and my stomach's growling, but I give Jordan a call on my office phone. Voice mail.

"Hey, Jor! Thought I might catch you but . . . oh, well, you're out. Hope you're having fun, sweetie. Just wanted to tell you how excited I am about you coming down here. See you in a few days!" I seal my message with a kiss, then kill the lights and head for the elevator.

Silent and dim, the Kult Ink offices after-hours are kind of creepy. In fact, this is the first moment since I've been in New York that I've felt so literally alone. Six floors below me are the teeming streets, the relentless hum of humanity. Yet up here it's desolate. I stab the elevator button impatiently — what's taking it so long?

Then a noise startles me. It's not the elevator awakening. It's coming from the other side of the office. "Who's there?" I say.

"Who's *there*?" The voice rebounds, but it's not an echo of my own. It's a male voice. I'm only wary for the nanosecond it takes me to recognize it.

"I don't know about *there*," I say, attitude on. "But *I'm* here."

"Me too," Gabe says. And just like that, he's beside me. The elevator takes eons — which doesn't bother me at all. There's a sci-fi feeling in the air, like me and Gabe aren't simply alone in Kult Ink reception but the last boy and girl on the planet. The semidarkness only makes me more hyper-aware of his presence. I see him: stark white of his T-shirt and teeth almost glowing, tanned face, brown hair, and indigo jeans blending in with the air. Yet I sense him more acutely than I see him, and I get the feeling it's the same for him. We both have that crackly, wired tension you get when you've been pulling long hours on a project. Mix in the surprise of discovering you're not alone — that abrupt intimacy, and the vague insecurity that comes with it. Thoughts of my hair, my breath, occur to me as I mark off the distance between us. Two feet? Three? Then, in one long-legged stride, Gabe closes the gap. Just to punch the elevator button? Or to be that much closer? He dips his head, and his curls fall into his eyes. "So what journalistic endeavor keeps you here so late?" he asks.

"Working on that Turpentine Cocktail assignment I was foolish enough to take on." Funny, how bright and alert I suddenly feel.

"I should be so foolish," Gabe says, sighing.

"Well, what had your nose to the grindstone?"

"Updating the public relations database," he says. "A dirty, not to mention brain cell–depleting job, but someone had to do it. Man, am I fried!"

The elevator arrives, wheezes open, and we step into the industrial iron cage.

Gabe stretches his arms over his head, then jumps twice, rattling the elevator — and me.

"Gabe, stop!" I shriek. "Don't do that!"

He gives me his trademark look — that snile, that smark. "What? You afraid mighty ape man will break spindly elevator?"

"Just stop," I say testily. Only not really testily. Sort of mock-testily. So he won't know what I'm really feeling. Which I can't quite identify myself. Except that it's tingly in the extremities and fluttery in the stomach and a little all-over achy that the ride to the bottom is a mere six flights. Anyway, he obeys. "Well, it might be brain cell–depleting, but at least you get paid," I point out.

"Yup," Gabe says. "I'm a wealthy man — so why don't you let me treat you to a late-night snack?"

It slides off his tongue so easily, so naturally, I don't even know what I'm saying when — easily, naturally — I say okay.

THE PERFECT GUY

Is he a mythical creature, a figment of fairy-tale Ken doll culture? Or does he exist, in all his sweet, smart, sexy, sensitive glory? And how will you recognize him when you see him?

Hanging out with another writer is like discovering chocolate. No offense to my other friends — back in Southie, here in New York — but Gabe just *gets* it. The impulse to put ideas across, with the permanence of ink on paper. The quest for words, not just words that convey meaning but words that rock with the rhythm of the sentence, like music.

"I had my first poems published in the third grade," Gabe tells me over falafel at this Middle Eastern eatery narrow as a shower stall. "Ow — that sounded so obnoxious."

"No, no, not at all!" Learning he's a poet confirms something I'd been hoping would peek out, a sensitive side, the soulful Gabe. It gives me the urge to reach across the table, but instead I just wave my pita. "You should be proud. It's so amazing to see your name in print, next to words you plucked from thin air and assembled like a puzzle. Not that I ever wrote poetry."

Gabe raises his eyebrows. "I thought all girls wrote poetry. Like iambic pentameter is chromosomal."

I give him a "not me" shrug. "I do have a flair for the dramatic," I say. "Sometimes I think about writing a novel. But journalism, I'm so drawn to it. Reality, but presented in a riveting way."

He nods, curls bouncing. "That's how I feel about it too. Music journalism, sure, but really investigative reporting. Hey, can I tell you something?" He leans over toward me, and whispers, "I can't go a day without reading *NYDP*."

I can't help but laugh. The *New York Daily Paper* is nothing but a few scraps of news sandwiched between celebrity scandal and sports. "God, Gabe, what's next — a subscription to *Us Weekly*?"

He doesn't seem to mind my taunting him; in fact, he leans in closer. "Oh, come on, Babylon," he says softly. "Are you saying you don't have any guilty pleasures?"

Wow, um, okay — two words have never been quite so loaded as "guilty" and "pleasure," especially coming from Gabe right now, under the spark of his eyes. I admit it, being with Gabe *is* a pleasure. As to guilty? Well, I'm supposed to be investigating his interest in Tabby, not flirting. Besides, I couldn't possibly undercut Tabby like that . . . at least not consciously. And with Jordan arriving this weekend! I avoid

Gabe's gaze to take a few long sips of water and try to get my head on straight.

"I'll have you know that my journalistic taste is beyond reproach! I've been reading the *Times* online every morning since I came to town," I insist, firmly putting an end to all subjects guilty and pleasurable. Except now my semi-slip into girl treason — flirting with another chick's crush — reminds me of something. "Hey, Gabe, can I ask you a hypothetical question?" I can see by his face he's taking me seriously. "Say you're on assignment, and it's a great story, you're really into it — but there's another story you feel more passionate about. A story you know really needs to get out there. Trouble is, your editor nixed it."

"Ooh, draconian!"

I could swim in his vocabulary.

"I feel the hypothetical pain," Gabe says. "You're on deadline for the one piece, but you can't stop thinking about the other."

I nod. It's like he's up in my head with me!

"What would I do?" He rubs his chin. "Well, to me the only way to banish obsession is to dig into it. You've got to follow your nose on the story that's consuming you — it won't just go away. But at the same time, of course, complete the other assignment. A lot of work, I know, but check it out. Best-case scenario, you show it to your editor, and she realizes how important it is. Second-best case, you pitch it someplace else, keep pitching until someone takes it. Worst-case? Even if everybody turns you down, you still benefit. Because the more you write, the better you get. And that's not hypothetical; that's the truth."

He is *so* right! Of course — I've *got* to pursue "Girls vs. Girls"! Maybe it would be presumptuous to write it, but if I research it, leaving no stone unturned, and outline it to the letter, then show Izzie, she'll recognize we have to expose *Orange* readers to it. Together, we can find just the right tone to get the message out there, but still keep it sounding *Orange*. Bonus? Getting two huge features together at the same time will doubly prove my drive and talent to Izzie! Plus, the two stories complement each other: *Orange* can run "Girls vs. Girls" in the Run Amok issue, and "Girls Helping Girls" as a follow-up. Oh my God — it's perfect! By now I must be beaming, because Gabe meets my eyes and smiles back.

Nothing could spoil this moment, not even our waiter stalking up with our check, plus two teeny cups and a small square of pastry. "On the house," he says. Translation: Eat up and get lost! It's late and he probably wants to go home.

"Watch out for that Turkish coffee," Gabe warns. "You'll be speeding all night."

I take the challenge. Think: hot bitter mud. But the nutty confection — Gabe calls it baklava — is so honey-drenched it balances the brew. Diligently I explore both tastes, lost in the experience, until I catch him watching me. I look up. "What?"

"You look different tonight," he says.

"Different?" Suddenly the whole timbre of what's been going on between us changes, and I study my coffee grinds, feeling self-conscious. "Oh. Maybe it's my hair." I pull absently at one of the springy coils.

"Yeah, that must be it. I really like the lightning-bolt part."

Lightning-bolt part! What a perfect description. But I wish he'd stop scrutinizing me . . . or maybe I wish he'd never stop. "Emmalee did it," I say. "She's so talented. With hair, clothes, décor, anything like that, she's incredible. All the Run Amoks — I got to say, they're almost preternaturally gifted." I am officially babbling now. "We'd better go, huh?" I stand up, collect my stuff. Gabe litters the table with bills. Once we're on the street I strive to find my equilibrium — and in a flash I figure out how.

"So, Gabe, I've been meaning to talk to you about something . . . some*one*," I say as we stroll toward Seventh Avenue. "Tabby." I pronounce her name firmly.

"Tabby? You're kidding me! This is cosmic!" he says. "I've been meaning to talk to you about Tabby too."

Oh. He has? Okay. Fine. "Well, then, how serendipitous that I brought her up," I say, surveying the enthralling

131

display of hammers in a hardware store window. I'm stalling, and I know it.

"It really is," Gabe says. "Because this is going to sound so middle school, but . . . well, I wanted to ask you, or tell you, because I know you guys are friends . . ."

Why doesn't he just come out with it!

"Well, the thing is, Finney has a massive crush on her. And he wanted me to ask you if you thought she thought he was cute or nice or cool or remotely appealing in any way, shape, or form."

That asthma attack I felt coming on miraculously disappears. "Finney? Likes Tabby?" I say. "Finney likes Tabby! Oh, Gabe, that's wonderful!"

I am busting to download this data. Despite her telling me she's into Gabe, when Tabby finds out Finney's sweating her, I'm sure she'll flip that script. After all, what does she really know about Gabe? Now, Finney — he'd be ideal for her. They're two of a kind, in fact, sort of bubbly and enthusiastic, and he's so smitten, he'd worship the ground Tabby walks on. Too bad it's so late when I slip into the suite — even Paulina is tucked in. Quietly I wash up and climb into bed, but my thoughts are like the Indianapolis 500 — and it's not just the Turkish coffee talking. Being with Gabe was so stimulating! But I push him out of my mind; I've done squat to plan my weekend with Jordan, and there are so many things

I want to show him. I doubt I get more than four hours sleep, but I still rise and (sort of) shine at seven to hit the pavement with Nae-Jo.

Should I tell her the great news? No, Tabby ought to be first to know. Besides, even though I've reached the point where I'm not eating Nae-Jo's dust, communicating while we run is not so doable. So here we are, neck and neck, when guess who sprints up to make it a three-way tie?

"Whoo!" Izzie tags Nae-Jo on the shoulder. "In case you thought an old girl didn't have the juice to keep up!" With silver stretchy-satiny shorts and a matching racer-back jog-top showing off her toned legs and summer tan, Izzie's like a Nike commercial in 3-D. Completing the scene? Copper, her gorgeous Irish setter, bounding along beside us.

At the fitness station, Izzie attacks the scaling wall with gusto, but soon enough she's sidetracked. "Well, hey there!" she hollers at a paunchy guy with a camera around his neck. "So you're ready to lose that jelly-belly, huh, Jeff?"

The photographer focuses; the shutter whizzes away. "Come on, Iz, you know my only exercise is elbow-bends." His voice is gruff as he gives her a distinct leer. "But I wouldn't miss the sight of you in your Judy Jetson jogging gear for all the distilled potatoes in Poland."

Izzie leaps off the wall to greet him. "Oh, Jeff — you don't want any pictures of me!" she insists, but keeps posing anyway. At this moment, it occurs to Nae-Jo that her dream photo op is on tap, and Izzie welcomes her into the frame. "Jeff, this is Nae-Jo Rodriguez, one of the girls who's kicking ass at *Orange* this summer. Nae-Jo, meet Jeff Pogachefsky from *NYDP*."

"Hey, Jeff!" Nae-Jo's stoked. Watching her and Izzie ham it up gives me mixed emotions. I don't want anyone taking my picture — not at this hour, looking like do-do. But the way they ignore me makes me feel worse than do-do. Somehow Izzie must sense this, since she waves me over.

"This is Babylon, another one of my girls with juice," she says. "Babylon's our Think! Editor — quite the wordsmith!"

I say hello, trying not to play connect the dots with the stains on the guy's grubby T-shirt. "Come on, honey, get in the shot," he says, ogling me.

Okay, he did *not* just call me honey.

"Indomitable editrix Izzie LaPointe and her mighty media fledglings!" cries Jeff. "Everyone smile and say *sexy*!"

Ugh! If I ever needed a shower after a run! I can't wait to scrub off that sleazoid's stare! Except Tabby exits the bathroom just as I'm heading in and I know this is my chance. "Tabby! I need to talk to you!" I tell her.

"Good. Talk," Nae-Jo says, scamming past me. But I can't even be mad, especially the way Tabby's eyes bug, like she knows what I have to say. She hauls me onto the sofa.

"Okay, tell me," she says. "Wait, wait — you're smiling!

I knew it! He likes me, doesn't he? When did you see him? What did he say! Oh my God!"

Tabby's near frenzy cues Paulina. A vision in fuzzy Elmo slippers, Fugazi T-shirt, and smudges of leftover eyeliner, she flops in one of the armchairs, yesterday's stale donut in one hand. "Jesus Christ, it's eight A.M.," she says, picking at sprinkles. "What's got Tabby in such a tizzy already?"

I look at Tabby to see if she cares who else listens. "Go, Babyl, spill!" she says. "I want the whole world to know."

Um, let's hope so. "Well, I was hanging with Gabe last night, and when I brought up your name, he said it was funny, because he was going to ask me about you too."

Clutching the collar of her robe, Tabby's about to fall into a full-on swoon. I'd better get through this fast. "Tabby, let me finish. He said he was going to bring you up because one of his friends really, really likes you."

Am I speaking Tunisian? Tabby stares at me blankly. "Um, excuse me, Babylon — I'm . . . not sure I . . ."

"Tabby," I say, "it's Finney. Finney is crushing on you."

"Finney!" she exclaims.

"The receptionist?" hoots Paulina, who is so not helping me out here. I throw her some tight-lipped scorn just as Emmalee enters the living room.

"Babylon Edison!" Em scolds. "Where in the world were you all night!" She's not helping much either.

"I'll tell you where she was!" Tabby says. "Stealing my

crush! What's *wrong* with you, Babylon?! I tell you I like Gabe so you turn around and go for him. I thought I could trust you!"

Paulina pounces — clearly enjoying this. "Not cool, Babylon. Not cool to Tabby, not cool to Gabe, not cool to Jason, not cool to anyone."

Emmalee looks at all of us quizzically, then says, "Pardon me, Paulina, but when did you become The Ethicist? And who in the world is Jason?"

How could this day be so messed up, and me not even showered yet?

"Babyl's boyfriend, Jason — but maybe she forgot all about him." Paulina's like a cat with a wriggling mouse beneath her paw.

This is ridiculous! "My boyfriend's name is Jordan, Paulina, and no, I did not forget about him."

"Then what were you doing with Gabe till all hours?" Tabby demands.

"Not your business, Tabby —" I cut my glare at Paulina before she can butt in. Emmalee sits in the other armchair, observing. "The point is, Tabby, Gabe told me that Finney likes you. He didn't mention his feelings one way or the other, but I can tell you right now he's not the kind of person to snake his friend's crush — and neither am I."

Nae-Jo, damp and in a towel, appears in the middle of the room. "What the — what I miss?" she wants to know.

"Finney's into Tabby, Tabby's into Gabe," Paulina fills her in, ticking off the goings on with sprinkle-sticky fingers, "and Babyl thinks we're all stupid enough to believe she and Gabe are purely platonic."

Nae-Jo whistles, as if somehow impressed. "Let me get this straight. Finney, the phone boy, wants to get with Tabby, but she likes the curly-haired egg-heady type . . . okay, got it. So what's Babyl's problem?"

"Shut up!" I scream. I do. I actually scream. "First of all, stop denigrating Finney. He pitches in as needed at all Kult Ink's magazines — he's very involved; Gabe told me so. Second, I am *not* cheating on Jordan — unlike Paulina I am capable of spending time with a guy without grinding up against him in a lust-induced stupor. And not that it's any of your beeswax, but Jordan and I are tight, we're good, and if we weren't, do you think he'd be coming down to New York to visit me this weekend? But since *everything* I do seems to be of collective Run Amok concern, then with your *kind* permission I'm going to take a goddamn *shower*!"

THE INCREDIBLE EXPLODING COUPLE

Boy hugs girl. Boy bugs girl. Girl goes ballistic and blows up. Fasten your seat belts — it's going to be a bumpy night!

A photo of Izzie and Nae-Jo appears on *NYDP*'s fabtastic Page 6 Thursday morning, and I cannot grumble that the icky paparazzi assiduously cropped me out. Complaint is impossible because by tomorrow my adorable, devoted boyfriend will be peppering me with kisses. My rant in the suite yesterday effectively got Paulina off my back, and seemed to at least partially convince Tabby that there's nothing going on between Gabe and me. Now that I've imparted the info about Finney, I'm staying in my lane. If Tabby decides to go for him, fine; if not, that's fine too.

My focus for the weekend will be my man! I refuse to even think about work either. Sure, taking on "Girls vs. Girls" as well as "Girls Helping Girls" is heaping a ton on my plate, but I feel really solid about my plan. Besides, after chilling with Jordan all weekend, I'll be refreshed and renewed, able to go after it like gangbusters.

"You sure you don't want to come to the screening?" Emmalee asks as she redoes her makeup in our room that evening. Tabby has passes for a film version of Edith Wharton's *The Fruit of the Tree*. I figure Em wants me to come mostly to make sure everything's cool between Tabby and me, after the blowup.

"No way, I've got work to do . . . on 'Girls Helping Girls.' " I still haven't told Em about my mission yet. "And I've got to e-mail Jordan — I can't believe I forgot to give him the address!" I hug my pillow to my chest. "I really am excited about seeing him, Em; just thinking about him makes me all . . . I don't know . . ."

"Would you rather call him?" she asks. "I could leave you my phone."

"You are the best!" I say, and she tosses it to me. I tap in his number before she's fully out the door.

"Babylon! Finally!" Jordan rarely gets agitated; he's the definition of laid-back. If he's hyper now, he's entitled. "Geez, I'm coming down tomorrow and I don't even know where you are," he says.

"Jordan, Jordan, I know — you're right," I say. "I have no excuse, except that I've been beyond busy. I'm really sorry, okay?"

The edge in his voice crumbles. "Well, you'll get to take it easy and have a nice long weekend," he promises.

Should it irk me that he doesn't even inquire *what* I've been so industrious about? That he expresses not one iota of interest in my work? That he assumes I can drop all my responsibilities just because he's coming? No, it shouldn't. We've been planning his visit since the day I learned I was coming to *Orange*.

"Well, I'm sure going to try," I say. "But you'll see when you get here, New York is so kinetic, relaxation isn't always an option."

"Oh, I bet I can make you relax. . . ." His tone turns husky now, and I roll over on my bed, facing the wall, Em's phone nestled against my ear. "Do you want me to tell you what I'm going to do?" he offers suggestively.

He starts going into detail, saying how much he missed me, how he can't wait to kiss me, all the kind of romantic stuff you think boys never say but they do when they really love you, and I'm lying in bed, reveling in every word — when all of a sudden Nae-Jo barges in, oblivious, and starts using Emmalee's bed as a trampoline.

"Ba-bee-lon! Ba-bee-lon! What up!"

"Um, Nae-Jo — I'm on the phone!"

"Well." Jump. "Get." Jump. "Off." Jump. She's acting like a two-year-old on too many jelly beans. "Come on, I snagged an invite to the Curzo party and you're my plus one!"

Ooh, Curzo's only the coolest skateboard company in both hemispheres. Their parties must be hot! And if Tabby's out with Emmalee, why shouldn't I hang with her roommate?

"Heyyyy, Babyl?" Jordan vies for my attention.

"Ohh, Jordan, sorry, sorry! Nae-Jo just came in and . . ."

"Arrggh! Damn it, Babylon, I thought we were having a conversation here!" he hurls the accusation — which instantly makes me mad.

"Look, Jordan, what do you want?" I snap, sitting up. I'm dimly aware that Nae-Jo's still in the room — she shuts up fast. "You know, my life is incredibly hectic right now, thank you so much for *not* asking, but all you can think about is Jordan McCormack!" I stand up, collecting myself — smoothing my shirt, searching for my sneakers.

"Babylon, please, you're right — I'm an asshole," Jordan tries to make amends. "It's just . . . I wish I was there already, with you. . . ."

"Oh, really?" I say, still pissed. "Look, Jordan — maybe you better not come."

"What?!" he cries. "Babylon, no! We've been planning this!"

"I hear you, Jordan . . . but things here . . . I'm just . . . I don't know. . . ." And I really don't. I don't know anything right now, except that if I'm not careful I could cry.

"Please," he says. "A) I'm a jerk and B) I love you and C) I really want to see you and D) we *will* have fun, whatever we do, no pressure, I just . . . Babylon, come on. . . ."

I listen to his appeal, one sneaker on, the other still MIA. "Okay," I say finally. "Got a pen?" I supply the data he needs to Mapquest his journey. He provides me with an estimated time of arrival, and we try to recapture some semblance of civility before we hang up.

Nae-Jo stares at me; I stare through her. "Looking for this?" She picks up my left sneaker, wedged against the dressing table between my bed and Emmalee's. She tosses it; I catch it and shove it onto my foot.

"Curzo soiree?" I say grimly. "Come on — let's go."

"Wow, Babylon, thanks!" Jordan digs through the bag of Curzo swag I picked up for him at the party last night. "*Par*kour? Um, what's that?"

We're sitting in the pizzeria near the *Orange* office — I'm turning Jordan on to his first New York slice. I'd been nervous all day, since we hung up kind of weirdly last night, but when I met him in Kult Ink reception I flew into his arms and knew everything was all right.

"Park*our*." If only Jordan had attended more French classes than he ditched, perhaps his pronunciation wouldn't be so off. "It's this French extreme sport. There was a party for it in DUMBO last night; all this stuff is typical swag."

Jordan laughs. "DUMBO? Swag? Babylon, speak English!"

I laugh too. Being with him just makes me so happy!

"So what's next on the agenda?" he asks.

I give him the dorm pass I'd prearranged for and a Post-It with the address of a nearby garage. "I know it's expensive, but you take your chances leaving the car on the street overnight," I say. "So just go downtown, park, drop off your stuff . . ."

"Wait, you're not coming with me?"

"Jordan, it's the middle of the afternoon! I have to go back to work," I explain.

"Oh, come on, blow it off, Babyl," he tempts me, lightly tickling the inside of my arm. "Your suite mates won't be there. . . ." He presses my wrist to his lips in a way that sends sparks down my spine. "Can't one of the other girls cover for you?"

"Jordan, I can't," I say, trying not to get exasperated anew over the fact that he has no concept of what it is I do. "But I'll be out the door at six, I swear."

He tries to play me with a pout, but it soon turns into a grin. "I'll be timing you," he says.

Despite my best intentions, I don't leave *Orange* till seven thirty. Fortunately back at the Dorm of Doom, I find the boom box blasting, a faint hint of weed under vanilla incense, and Paulina — pal that she is — entertaining my boy. I only wish she would have put a shirt on to do so.

"Hey, Babyl — you didn't tell me Jordan had such killer taste in music!" she shouts from the sofa in flimsy cutoffs and red bra.

Jordan jumps up with a goofy grin. Good thing he's a little high — he doesn't realize I'm so late. We kiss deeply,

and I admit I make a bit of a show for Paulina's benefit —
staking claim in case she's got anything stewing in her twisted
little brain. "Mmmm!" I say, holding Jordan's face in my
palms, drinking in the sight of him. "Let me just change
my shirt and we can go out."

Dinner is amazing. Lasagna is one of Jordan's favorite
dishes, so I lead him to Little Italy, this place like a grotto, all
rustic and candlelit. Afterward, we make out on practically
every corner between the restaurant and the dorm, then
adjourn to Paulina's room. She told us to feel free; she'll be
spending the night with her latest flame, Thaniel (she's been
seeing him almost a week — it must be love!).

Side by side, we inhale each other. Then, in no particular
order, I do the things that make him moan. The chain of tiny
kisses, the taunting stab and swirl of tongue, the fluttering
touches to his chest, his stomach, stopping short at the top of
his jeans. He takes all that he can take before grabbing both
my hands in his, pressing me onto my back, holding me there
with all his strength, and now it's his turn — to nuzzle and
lick until I'm the one wriggling and murmuring, spine arch-
ing . . . Just for the record, Jordan and I don't have sex. Well,
we do — it's all sexual activity in my book — but corny as it
sounds we've made a pact to lose our technical virginity to
each other a little less than a year from now, post–senior
prom. I'm not sure we'll hold out, but so far we've been

managing to get each other pretty intoxicated with all the other things we do.

The next morning we sleep late, and when we emerge, we find that Emmalee and Tabby have conspired on breakfast. Em must have fully drilled it into Tabby that I'm not the devil incarnate, or else she just can't help herself from being social, since she's back to her effusive self.

"Oh, Jordan, it's so nice to meet you — Babylon prattles on about you nonstop," she says, which is flattering to Jordan if not exactly true. "How are you guys going to spend the day?"

I spell out our itinerary. "I thought we'd do the Museum of Natural History, since I can't see Jordan enduring the Met," I say. "Then Central Park, then maybe we'll walk on Fifth Avenue a while."

Emmalee nibbles daintily on a croissant, pats her lips. "Just don't exhaust yourselves too much," she says. "That is, if we're still all going out tonight."

"Sure!" Jordan says. "I can't wait to take a bite out of Big Apple nightlife."

He winks to show he's trying to be funny, but the way he says it makes me wince inwardly anyway. "Well, we could just go to a movie," I say. "We don't have to do anything major."

Emmalee looks taken aback. "But Babylon, tonight's the Urban Jungle Ball!" she reminds me. "It's the most exclusive party in town, and we're all on the list. Izzie called Emilio personally!"

"Wall-to-wall celebrities and supermodels!" chimes in Tabby. "Nobody who's anybody is even going to the Hamptons this weekend. Jordan won't want to miss that!"

"Well, this weekend is supposed to be about us — I don't want to lose my boyfriend in a sea of supermodels," I say lamely, suddenly dreading the party and not knowing why. "Besides, we're not the fabulous fashion-party types."

"Hey, speak for yourself, Babyl!" Jordan says, standing up to strike a pose, hand on hip, bagel extended haughtily. "I can be fabulous!"

The girls giggle, and I smile weakly — but I don't have the best feeling about this.

Maybe I'm wrong; maybe the Jungle Ball will be great. During our lovely but loooong afternoon, Jordan and I speed-shop through H&M. He picks up a cool new shirt, and I get an upgrade on my old reliable party dress — a polka-dotted retro-style frock with a tight bodice and flared skirt. Back at the dorm, Emmalee tells us how cute we look — the style maven seal of approval — as she snaps pics with her camera phone.

Paulina and her date swing by so she can change, and Jordan seems glad he's not the only guy in the room.

"Hey, Daniel," he says.

"Thaniel." Thaniel corrects him. Guess he gets that a lot. "Short for Nathaniel. Because, you know, man — everyone's a Nate."

Jordan shoots me a quick smile, and I get the feeling this encounter will make the rounds back up in Southie; I can already hear Fiona asking me, "So, Babyl, how's *Thaniel*?"

Then Jordan insists on driving. All of us. Seven people in a Volkswagen Cabriolet. "What it costs in a cab will still be less than putting the car back in the lot," I attempt to reason with him. To no avail. No one complains about the tight squeeze, though — in fact, everybody's acting like passengers in a circus clownmobile — but I feel all smushed and ruffled by the time we reach the party.

As Tabby predicted, the famous have flocked — and to my horror, Jordan develops acute celebrititis, finding it necessary to speak to every star he recognizes. Just when I thought it couldn't get any worse, he starts collecting autographs.

After we're there a while, Izzie motions for us to join her and meet our host, the fashion designer Emilio Dazza. *Please, Lord, don't let Jordan do anything dumb in front of my boss!* That's my silent prayer.

"Babylon, your boyfriend's so handsome," Izzie says sweetly. "He looks like a Kennedy! Of course, Emilio cannot let an attractive man into his atelier without trying to transform him into the next Alex Lundqvist."

"You mean Henrik Lundqvist," Jordan says.

And my mind screams: *No, Jordan, no — do not be correcting Izzie, especially when you have no clue what you're talking about!*

Izzie and Emilio snicker. Jordan laughs too. I seem to be the only person immune to the hilarity. "Not that I'd mind though!" Jordan shoves his foot in further. "You want to get me a contract with the Rangers, Mr. Dazza, I'll take it!"

It's my cue to intervene. "No, Jordan, they mean Alex Lundqvist, the supermodel, not Henrik Lundqvist, the hockey player," I say. Laughter erupts once more, though I still fail to grasp what's so damn funny.

Once that mortifying scene plays out, I tell Jordan as calmly as I can that I'm ready to leave. The elevator descends about half a floor before it dawns on Jordan that something is amiss. "Babylon?" he asks. "Are you all right?"

Now this could go two ways. I could show him how that girl in *The Exorcist* has nothing on me, or I could opt for the silent treatment, icily informing him how badly he embarrassed me without uttering a solitary syllable. But something else, something unexpected, happens. The elevator opens, I step onto the sidewalk — and I burst into tears. I'm crying because, angry as I am, I realize that Jordan did nothing intentional to displease me. On the contrary, in fact. He bought a new shirt he didn't really need so he'd look his best — for *me*. He crammed everyone into his Cabriolet to do a nice thing — for *my* friends. He got starstruck at the party because he was agog — by the kind of people *I* run with these days. And he elicited laughter from two New York luminaries — including *my* boss — without even caring that they were laughing at him, not with him.

"Babylon, Babylon! What is it? What's the matter? What did I do?" he says.

I'm bawling too hard to explain, but I try to anyway, and finally, he seems to comprehend. "So I made a fool of myself — is that it?" he says. "Babylon, it's okay, really. Big deal! I don't care!"

No, I'm wrong: He comprehends nothing. "But I do!" I wail. "I care! These people, they think you're an idiot. And I'm you're girlfriend! So what does that make me?"

We're at the car now. It's started to drizzle. Passersby pick up their pace, rushing to get where they have to go with hair and makeup intact, shoes clacking and voices rising. Jordan unlocks the passenger side, and I get in. He takes his seat behind the wheel and stares out at the asphalt as it turns shiny and slick. Slowly my sobs subside.

"I don't know what to tell you, Babylon," he says after an endless minute. "I'd apologize, but I can't, because I was just being myself." He lets out a long sigh. "I'm me, and you're you — but the problem is, you're not the same person. Being here, this job, these people . . . you've changed, Babylon. I haven't. I'm still me." He puts the key in the ignition and starts the car, pulls away from the curb. He still hasn't looked at me, and his eyes remain on the road when he says, "The only thing I'm sorry about is that you don't seem to like who I am anymore."

WHO'S THAT GIRL?

Just when you thought you knew someone, she goes and pulls a 180. . . .

Eggshells everywhere! In the dorm, at the office, all the Run Amoks are acting oh-so-considerate ever since Jordan left. Offering a shoulder. An ear. Half a dozen cupcakes from Treat Me Nice, this SoHo bakery that I swear puts crack in the frosting. My friends think I should talk. Because that's what chicks do — we talk. Well, call me the Anti-chick. Of course, I appreciate it — the support and sympathy, the sugar — but really, I'm good.

Okay, not *good,* but not a wreck. Rightfully upset, since I don't even know what's what, if Jordan and I are broken up or on hiatus or just licking our wounds. We really didn't talk that night either. There was nothing to say, or too much to say, so we went to bed, trying not to touch. Come the clear light of day, I woke to this illusory sweetness — we'd managed to cuddle up during the night — but no matter how physically perfect it felt I knew we had crossed a line. For a few minutes I lay in his arms, savoring him — his strength, his skin, the structure of his face and his warm, even breath. Then it became unbearable. Carefully I disentangled myself, but as soon as I slipped away, Jordan reached for me and, finding nothing but sheets and air, opened his eyes.

"Babylon . . ."

It occurred to me that might be the last time I'd hear him say my name.

He didn't stick around on Sunday. What was the point? He was right — I had changed. For better? For worse? Forever? We don't make up, we don't break up; the best we can do is agree to take a break. To simply say good-bye — kiss good-bye, yes, a lingering, all-is-not-lost kiss good-bye — and wait till summer's over to sort it all out.

Of course, there was no escaping Fiona, who IM'd me as soon as she caught wind, through big-mouth Ben.

fiona525: babyl! r u ok?

babyl: yeah, guess so.

fiona525: what tha ^$%@&#*! happened?

babyl: don't know! things just weird here. 2 much pressure? long distance = hard! ☹

fiona525: did you fight?

babyl: sort of . . . u see him? he ok?

fiona525: no & ben not saying much. this is nuts! babyl, get yr butt back here!

I swirl the thought around my brain. All of August, a million adventures, awaits me here. But I couldn't tell Fiona that.

fiona525:   look, I'm just going to blurt: i don't trust teri around jordan! when this gets out, she'll be all over him!

That made me feel like there was a hook in my heart. Eyes closed, I could visualize it, could see myself carefully extracting the hook and throwing it over a cliff, into the pounding surf. Eyes open, I felt minutely better.

babyl: teri's got to do what she's got to do. so does jordan. And so do i.

"Babyl? I need your opinion in the fashion closet . . . if you can spare a moment . . . ?"

Emmalee's seeking *my* style counsel? Hmm, no doubt this is just her two P.M. sanity check — it's three days since Jordan left, and the Run Amoks still have me under tight surveillance. Whatever. It's Em, so I'm up. The fashion "closet" is practically the size of our suite at the Dorm of Doom. Packed with clothes on rolling racks, shelves of shoes, cubbies crammed with accessories, it resembles no closet in the regular world, not even Paris Hilton's regular world. I'll be happy if my first apartment is this big.

"What do you think of these?" Gossamer-thin dresses dangle weightlessly from hangers. "Seasonless dressing is such the fashion zeitgeist now," Em says, "but I'm not sure — too flimsy for winter? Because I also have these — come, look, they're Dolly & Stone. The fabrics have a bit more substance, and they're kind of Goth, which is cool."

Looks like I missed the previews. "Em, you want to bring me up to speed here?" I say. "What are these dresses for?"

She taps her forehead. "Oh, Babyl, I'm so scattered, sorry," she says. "They're for 'Come As You Are.' The shoot's next week and I am so far from pulling it together."

Okay, but I'm still a few clues short. "I don't get it, Emmalee." I stroke one of the clingy, Goth-y dresses — it's feminine, but tough, and I could see myself sporting it with some lace-up boots and a studded choker. Whoa — did I really just flash on that? Seems like after a month in New York, a sense of style beyond the most basic has seeped in by osmosis. "This one gets my vote — but clarity, please. I mean, aren't you supposed to come as you are to 'Come As You Are?' Doesn't designer gear defeat the purpose?"

Emmalee frowns. "That's one of the things that's got me so frazzled," she says. "I had an impromptu audience with Izzie this morning. She told me all these companies were sending clothes, and when I expressed confusion, she put it to me like this. . . ."

This is where Emmalee goes into an Izzie impersonation, smiling like a hundred-watt bulb, accenting for emphasis.

"Emmalee, Emmalee, *Emmalee* — 'Come As You Are' is *genius* as a *concept,* but these girls we've chosen, their wardrobes are probably limited, right? Now, we don't want to foster bad feelings — that wouldn't be very *Orange.* And this shoot, it's a fantasy-come-true for them, yes? Really, Emmalee, if someone told you to come as you are, and you could either pick from your own old, outdated, worn-out stuff or fabulous, brand-new designer stuff, which way would you go?"

I'm about to applaud — the girl has Izzie down!

"Well, I was this close to telling Izzie that I don't consider my wardrobe to be outdated or worn-out, but then I thought about the average girl, and realized she's absolutely right," Em says, switching back to her own voice. "Except now I have to sort through all these clothes to make some preselects, because if I let the girls paw through everything on shoot day, it will be chaos, pure chaos! And I've got so much else on my mind as it is. Like this photographer Paulina wants to use — she's very good, a student at the High School of Art and Design, but what a diva! And the permits for shooting at Coney Island — so many rules and regulations. Plus, what if it rains?!"

She slumps against a table heaped with hats and scarves;

I lean alongside her, start offering solutions. We're making headway when Matumba intrudes. "I'm here to inform you that Izzie just approved the 'Beauty and the Brawn' layouts," she tells Emmalee as if every word has nails in it. "She's in Create! right now, if you want to see."

Em doesn't bother with Matumba's attitude. "Babyl, come on — you can see John Henry!"

We race down the hall to Create!, where the whole department gathers at a long table, oozing over the layouts — all but one of them convincingly. Slouching at the far end, Paulina barely feigns interest. She's gnawing a pencil like a wood chipper, and if this were a cartoon, her face would be green with envy.

"Oh, *Emmalee*! Just *look*!" Izzie is virtually paroxysming with delight. "I had a vision of you in this shoot, and when I have a vision, I have a *vision*!"

Em and I crowd around for a peek — and I gape. I mean, yes, Emmalee's beautiful, that's been established. But in this picture, with John Henry's strapping (sorry, but that *is* the word!) arms encircling her, she looks like a different person. No longer a sprite or a princess but a goddess, with all the smoldering power the word implies. With her makeup — smudgy eyes, tinted lips, naked cheeks — and tousled, tumbling mane of peach-gold flame (not the neat coifs Emmalee spins up for herself), it takes a second to register that it's even her.

"Oh . . ." Emmalee says, her head tilting slightly, her voice lilting strangely, something indecipherable in her smile. "Is . . . that . . . me?"

The snort is stifled, morphs into a cough, but I know what it means and who it's coming from. I catch Paulina shifting her weight from hip to hip, then fix my attention back on the layouts. "Whoever she is," I say, "we better put out an APB warning the men of the world."

Emmalee looks at me, and we both bust up laughing. Izzie joins in, slinging us into a three-way huddle-hug. "And check it out, Emmalee — this isn't even the best part," she says. "Diego, the photographer, he showed your contact sheets to the top booker at Delish. You're just a few negotiations away from a modeling contract."

Emmalee turns speechless at that, which is just as well, because Izzie isn't finished. She lavishes praise on Emmalee, then the Run Amok program, then girls with juice everywhere — her voice soaring, her teeth flashing, her eyes defying the fluorescent fixtures above our heads. Then she declares: "We should all go out and celebrate!"

Who all? I wonder.

"Matumba!" she bellows, but the girl seems to have vanished, so Izzie turns to me. "Babyl, help me out and find Matumba, tell her to clear my deck . . . and then . . . what do you think? Mongolian barbecue? Argentinean steakhouse? No-o-o, something more festive . . ." She snaps her fingers. "Tapas! Go on, Babylon, tell Matumba to reserve a table for six at Tapateria, and then go tell — oh, Paulina, you're already here, great — go give Tabby and Nae-Jo the 411."

Dinner is . . . interesting. Tapateria is this cavernous, noisy place with long tables, everyone seated communal-style. But Izzie wants a reserved table so it can be "just us," and what Izzie wants, Izzie gets; a private section has been cordoned off for our group. I've never had tapas before — nothing but appetizers and no main dish, so you eat for hours without feeling like you've had an actual meal.

The sangria's flowing too. If Izzie deliberates about ordering wine for minors, I can't see her mull it over. "A pitcher of the white sangria, six glasses, *por favor*," she tells the waiter without a flicker of concern. It seems like one more way to bond us to her and show that she considers us adults.

I haven't touched alcohol since my last night in Southie — not backstage at the Hammerstein, not at Emilio Dazza's atelier — but tonight I indulge. Something to take the edge off after the whole mess with Jordan, and all the work I've been churning out. Besides, the chilled wine with chunks of fruit is yummy — it doesn't taste like it could get you drunk. And, what the hell, *Orange* is buying.

"Emmalee, what did your parents say when you told them you're about to rule the modeling world?" Izzie asks.

Emmalee puts down her fork, chews, swallows, speaks.

"Oh, I haven't had a chance to call them yet — but I don't think my mom would approve."

Izzie sips her wine, shakes her head. "Au contraire," she says. "I happen to know, Emmalee, that your mom's a former pageant queen — oh, yes, we researched all of you! — so she couldn't possibly object. Especially since modeling is *so* much cooler than beauty contests. Not to mention the pay is off the charts!"

Emmalee pushes some octopus around her plate. "Well, for my family, money is not an issue," she says.

"Ah, well," Izzie says langourously. "You'll have to settle for glory and fame."

Without missing a beat, Em volleys back. "Oh, I doubt it will come to that." She puts her palm to her heart, pledging. "Not that I don't value the opportunity, because naturally I do, and you're so wonderful, Izzie, to believe in me." It's like Emmalee's shaking confectioners' sugar onto each syllable. "But it's obvious that I hardly meet the height requirements."

Check, I think, wondering if anyone else perceives this conversation as a kind of oral chess match.

"You might think so," says Izzie, grinning over her wineglass, "but I spoke to Felidia Connocetta at Delish myself. And you know what she said? 'Oh, EEEzie,' — she's Italian, Felidia is — 'I love that she is tiny! Tiny is the new tall!'"

Checkmate!

Emmalee cedes with a tight smile, and Izzie accepts her

victory with a broad one, signaling the waiter for another pitcher. Dinner discussion turns to bands and movies, celebrity gossip — and I don't know how much sangria we go through, but by dessert, we're sloshed. Izzie basically pours us into the Town Car, then hails a taxi for herself. Everything's copasetic on the drive to the dorm, but once we're in the suite things get ugly — the kind of ugly that's bound to occur when five girls who've been swilling wine simultaneously feel their bladders about to burst.

"You mind, supermodel?" Paulina hip-checks Emmalee roughly at the bathroom door.

"Yes, in fact, I do mind!" Emmalee's pissed, all pretense of politesse vanished.

"TFB!" Paulina, the epitome of class, yanks down her pants and underwear and sits while the rest of us Run Amoks dance the pee-pee pogo. "Why don't you just squat over a teacup, Miss Tiny is the New Tall?"

"Shut up, Paulina!" I say.

"No, *hurry* up, Paulina!" says Tabby.

"Yeah, before I pull you off there," says Nae-Jo. "I got to go, serious!"

Paulina laughs and leans over sideways on the "throne," trying to smack at Emmalee, standing by the sink. But between her wasted state and clumsy position, she topples over, bracing herself with one hand on the tile floor. It takes Paulina about three seconds to regain her balance.

Unfortunately for her, it takes Emmalee only two to snatch a tube of toothpaste off the sink, flip up the cap and squeeeeeeeeeeze!

"Oh! Oh!! OH!!" cries Tabby. Nae-Jo and I are flat-out stupefied. Toothpaste is flying, mostly all over Paulina's face and hair. Man, Rob Zombie and Marilyn Manson and Ozzy Osbourne are kicking themselves for not being here to record the sound of hell that erupts from Paulina. In full roar, she leaps up, lunging for Emmalee, forgetting that her jeans are around her ankles. She stumbles against the sink and slides to the floor, where she thrashes and writhes and seems to foam at the mouth — but no, that's not rabies, just Crest Whitening Formula.

Calmly, Emmalee steps around her, lowers her drawers, and sits daintily while Paulina clambers to her knees. Nae-Jo and I think the same exact thing at the same exact instant, rushing in to drag Paulina out before she can attack Emmalee, who finishes up, flushes, rises, and smiles. "Next?" she says.

"I COULD NOT TELL THE TRUTH!"

To spill or not to spill? That is the question. Find out what happens when a girl has honesty on the tip of her tongue — and it gets stuck. . . .

This is my first hangover, and although I have nothing to compare it to, I know it's a whopper. My eyelashes hurt, okay? Only forget what they say about misery loving company. Us Run Amoks can barely look at each other as we drag ourselves around the suite in a daze, trying to get it together for what promises to be a nightmare of a workday.

Natalie takes one look at me and understands, dosing me first with a liter of water, then a bagel (a few bites is all I can manage; chewing is painful), followed by three Tylenol and, finally, coffee. She's being cool about it all, no lecture on the evils of teenage boozing, but when I let slip that Izzie was behind the debauchery, her face pinches and pales.

"That woman is unconscionable!" Natalie blows up.

Our eyes lock then, both of us knowing we've said too

much of the wrong thing. Subtly, seamlessly, the look segues into one of "your secret's safe with me if mine's safe with you," and we cast our eyes away, turning on our computers.

The pounding headache and general malaise gradually fade as I keep sipping H_2O; by noon, after inhaling a grilled cheese, I'm pretty much back to normal. Still, thinking about Think! is a challenge, and I've got something to settle. Ergo:

To: e.roberts@orange.com, p.locke@orange.com,
t.sincowicz@orange.com, nj.rodriguez@orange.com
From: b.edison@orange.com
Subject: Run Amok meeting

Hey guys —

We need to talk. All of us. Because last night's incident didn't "just happen," it wasn't random, and we can't blame the sangria. It's been stewing. And if we don't get real about it, something like that could happen again. We don't want that. We're the original Run Amoks, the ultimate girls with juice. So tonight. Seven P.M. at the Dorm of Doom. Please be there.

Thanks —

Babyl

By seven-oh-one we're all assembled in the living room. Panic strikes — this may well be the stupidest idea I've ever had. Too late now — I summoned this congress, time to step up and lead it.

"Look, I'm just going to get this out, and then maybe you guys'll have something to say, and hopefully, when we're done, we can regain some of the unity and sisterhood that this program is supposed to be about."

A muffled hoot, a sigh, a rustle of crossing thighs. Not exactly the warm reception I was angling for. "Okay, so we're all smart and talented, and I think we all admire that in us. But something happened, pretty much from the jump, to screw that up. You know what I'm talking about. The column. We all want it, and we're all worthy, but only one of us can have it . . . and I think that's destroying us.

"It's one thing to do your best, try your hardest, but when it turns us into haters, that's messed up. Last night wasn't just about a certain person being jealous that another certain person will have her picture in the magazine. It was about a certain person possibly being Izzie's favorite, a slam dunk for the column. I know what I'm saying, too, because I know how I felt that day on the running path with Izzie, Nae-Jo, and me, and it was not cute." I set my gaze on Nae-Jo. "It was horrible! I love that Nae-Jo's a superior athlete, and a girl with juice, but thinking that Izzie likes her best, it killed me inside.

"So let's just cop to it, okay — and make a pact to cut it out. Because Izzie's going to pick who she's going to pick, and for all we know she's looking to see how we're handling all this. Maybe the greatest test of our merit isn't who produces the best section but who shows the best sports-chick-ship. After all, you guys, our whole reason for being here this summer is to put out the best damn issue of *Orange* ever — and to do it as a team. And the only way we can do that is by being honest."

Ooh, that was a mouthful. Is anyone feeling me? The expressions and postures the Run Amoks sat down with haven't changed much. But the strength of my convictions empowers me; I'm speaking the truth as I see it and that's righteous, liberating.

"Are you *done*?"

Actually, I'm not. Since *screeeech*, I just realized that I, too, am guilty of deviously vying for Izzie's favor. All this talk of honesty, yet I haven't told a soul about undertaking "Girls vs. Girls" — and what's that but a stealth stab at proving *I'm* the girl with the most juice? As long as Operation Double Duty stays clandestine, it's not cool. Only by coming clean can I show the Run Amoks there are limits to how far *this* girl will go to get what she wants. And I intend to, I do — except apparently Paulina feels I've held the floor long enough.

"Because really, Babylon, the way you speechify, you

ought to run for president." She draws out of her lazy sprawl to sit up straight — a preamble, no doubt, to a counter-rant. "I know I'd vote for you."

Huh? What? Paulina's on my side?

"Hey, I know I'm a 'certain person,' and you're right," she says. "I was shitty to Emmalee, and not just my regular, knee-jerk reaction shitty, but particularly shitty, AP shitty. And why? Because Emmalee's rich and well-bred and perfect — and let's not forget oh-so-photogenic?" She slits her eyes on Em, holds them there. "No. Because I take my stand against the princess complex by being me, in all my brash, obnoxious glory. But the idea that Izzie could prefer Emmalee to me?" She shudders for effect.

"Izzie's my heroine, and since I've been here, I've felt like she's my *friend,*" Paulina goes on. "And the thought of being dumped by her, for one of you, any of you . . . that sucks to the bone." She takes a breath, shakes her head. "So, first up, Emmalee, I'm sorry. Even though I'll still be picking toothpaste out of my hair when I'm thirty. And second, third, and fourth, I apologize to the rest of you guys for any over-the-top nastiness I might have hurled your way. I'll try to be better . . . and, well . . ." She shrugs. "That's it."

Tabby is out of the armchair and all over Paulina like a shot. "Oh, Paulina! Of course we forgive you!" she says. "And Izzie *is* your friend; she loves you and respects you and thinks you have gobs of talent. And so do I!"

Nae-Jo leaps into the lovefest next — in her own way. "Yo, you know what? If Izzie gives you the column instead of me, I won't hurt you *too* bad." She punches Paulina lightly on the arm.

Nice, but Emmalee's exoneration is what Paulina seems to crave — and naturally, Em steps up. "Last night was as much my fault as yours, Paulina," she says. "What I did was uncalled for. All I can attribute it to is, well, everything Babylon's been talking about. I've been jumping through hoops of fire to please Izzie — the modeling thing, and trying to make 'Come As You Are' a masterpiece. But one thing's for certain — having you there to art direct the shoot guarantees it will be great."

Paulina cocks her head. "Really? You think so?"

Emmalee smiles beatifically. "Of course," she says. "You're an enormous talent, Paulina."

"Thanks — you are too." Paulina looks around the room. "And by the way, any of you want to come to Coney Island, I'm sure Em and I can find something for you to do," she says, then adds, "Feel free to take this to mean that we're begging you!"

Wow, this is turning out better than I expected. "Well, since you're begging," I say. "I'll be there!"

"Me too!" says Tabby.

"Yeah, okay, count me in," says Nae.

Run Amok honor united, yeah! I'm so proud of us. Proud,

but pooped. The day's draining hangover has taken its toll, and we're all ready to turn in early. It's not till I'm in bed that I remember I never did tell all about Operation Double Duty — I toss around on that like it's lumps in the mattress.

"Hey, Em?" I say when I hear her come in. "Something's bothering me." I lift onto an elbow, study the shadows.

"You want to talk about it?" Emmalee asks, stifling a yawn.

"I do," I say, and give her the crib sheet version of my plan.

"Babyl, I think it's a great idea," Em says. "You have nothing to lose, in any event. But I wouldn't broadcast it if I were you."

Head nestling into the sweet spot on my pillow, brain urging me to hit the OFF switch, I struggle against sleep. "Hmm?" I ask hazily. "Why not?"

Emmalee's voice sounds faraway yet firm. "Because I'm me," she says, "and they're *them*."

YOU DO THE MATH

Here's a geometry problem for you: What do you get when boy likes girl, girl likes other boy, and other boy likes other girl . . . ?

The lions of the Serengeti could take lessons from Tabby Sincowicz. It's the second week in August, all her "Next Big Thing" stories are due, and she hasn't done half the interviews yet, which is why she's stalking me. Too bad. The Run Amoks may be a team but I refuse to take on any more of her responsibilities. Fortunately I can close the office door and hide out. Unfortunately there's no ducking e-mail. Tabby dings my in-box.

A simple "no" will not suffice. And so I type:

Tabby, there are plenty of able-bodied interns up in here you can assign. The Amuse! intern Jazmin, for instance? Or Matumba? How about Finney? Or Gabe; he's dying to write.

My in-box keeps quiet so I guess I pointed her in the right direction. In fact, I'm blissfully undisturbed until late afternoon — an e-mail that gives me the grins.

b —

u rock! i *know* u had something to do with t giving me an assignment. ur the only one @ *orange* who knows how bad i want 2 write! i owe u 1. coffee or something? feel like it's been a while . . .

— g

It has been a while. One week, five days, and approximately seven hours since we stood on a Chelsea street corner contemplating the potential coupling of Tabby and Finney. Since then, and the disastrous weekend with Jordan that followed, I've been keeping a low profile, especially as far as Gabe's concerned. Still, it makes me happy that he knew I had a hand in his writing for *Orange*. I'm not ready to see him yet, so I send a noncommittal "glad I could help" reply. I just hope he doesn't live to regret the hookup. No doubt Tabby will require many evening revision sessions. *Not your problem, Babyl,* I remind myself. Gabe's a resourceful boy; let him deal with Tabby, put her on the path to Finney himself. Forcefully I push all thoughts of that particularly sticky love triangle out of my mind.

And they stay away — until Friday, and "Come As You Are."

A lot of things go into a location shoot, but, literally, the biggest one is the motor home — a tricked-out rental with hair and makeup stations, changing areas, a bathroom, and room for a platoon of primp personnel. Our fashion show on wheels is packed to capacity — five real-girl models, five Run Amoks, two stylists, one senior Stun! staffer (Marguerite, who appears to be napping rather than supervising), and one photographer (with the divaesque name of Galaxie). Everyone's jabbering at once, but only the stylists are actively engaged.

Nae-Jo gives me a sly look. "You think anyone would notice if I got gone?"

There's a bikini under her clothes and a boogie board under her arm. It's not like we Run Amoks have been given a single thing to do so far, so all I do is shrug.

"Want to come?" Nae-Jo whispers. "You can borrow my board."

I'm tempted. This is Coney Island: sun, sand, ocean, boardwalk, rides — and here I am cooped up in a trailer. But just then Emmalee calls out: "Babyl? Tabby? Nae-Jo? *Someone*?"

Nae-Jo goes AWOL, but Tabby and I stick around to learn the secrets of styling. We duct-tape a hem. We stuff paper into shoes that are three sizes too big, and similarly pad a bra with socks. We tie a few strategic knots in a silk scarf until — ta-da! evening bag! We put safety pins where no safety pins have gone before. It's more MacGyver than glamour, but the girls are getting gorgeous, and the transformations are pretty impressive.

"I hate to ask . . ." Emmalee beguiles.

"No job too small," I say, meaning it. She's totally in her element today, running the show, and I'm happy to be of use.

"We miscalculated on beverage supply, and nothing's worse for the complexion than dehydration," she says. "Can you and Tabby find a deli and get as much water as you can carry?"

It's the chore I've been waiting for! A chance to check out Coney Island. Although what I peep upon exiting the motor home is a different kind of thrill than the one I expected.

"Ohhh! Hi, Gabe! You made it!" Tabby flits over, not the least bit surprised to see him and ignoring the fact that he's not alone. "I'm so glad! Isn't this a lovely day for a shoot? Ooh, look, isn't that the Cyclone? It's supposed to be the scariest roller coaster in the whole world!"

Finney just stands there — puppy-eyed, love-struck. "Hey, Finney," I say. "What brings you to Brooklyn?"

"Tabby . . ." he murmurs, as if that explains everything.

"Hey, Babyl, what up?" says Gabe. Damn if that boy isn't browner than me — he must have the kind of skin that tans easily.

"Oh, mousse, mascara, cleavage — you know, girl stuff. So did you guys confuse our motor home for the Coney Island fun house?"

Gabe smirks his smirk. "Tabby said we could photo assist," he says.

"Hi, Tabby . . ." says Finney — slack-jawed, crush-drunk.

"Oh, hello, Finney." Could Tabby be more terse? "Gabe, we're on a drink run. Did you happen to spy a deli on your way from the subway?"

He lifts his arm, to point, I think — but Tabby grabs hold like it's the last chicken wing in the Colonel's bucket. Finney and I fall in behind them, and I give up trying to talk to him. This usually chatty guy has Tabby fever, bad! As we're coming back with water, we see that the motor home has gone to our first location, so we hoof it to Astroland, Coney Island's historic theme park. Paulina positions our real-girl models on the Teacup Ride, and as hairstylist and makeup artist make final adjustments, Galaxie offers her a glimpse through the lens.

"Holy crap!" Paulina says. "That is *hot!*"

Then it's *whirr-whirr-whirr!* The camera starts snapping. Finney and Gabe jump into the fray for Paulina and Galaxie; Tabby and I are at Emmalee's command. The order of the moment? To incite, arouse, and ignite the models.

"This is a *party!*"

"This is *your* party!"

"Your crush just asked you to dance!"

"But you're too busy dancing with your girls!"

"Hands in the air! Shake that thing!"

"Whoo-hoo!"

Since they're not professional models, it takes a while for the girls to get their vogue on — about thirty seconds. Onlookers gather, and Paulina drafts Gabe and Finney into crowd control. After a few quick rolls of film, Galaxie shouts, "Got it! Come on! Next setup!" and we race into the motor home to prep for the next shot.

The guys are ousted, of course, while the models change. Gabe tugs my T-shirt and jerks his head in a "follow me" gesture. Finney sits — besotted, bewildered — on the motor home steps while Gabe hustles me to the other side.

"What's the deal?" he demands. "Am I in a *Twilight Zone* episode or what? Tabby's all over me like bling on Beyoncé, and Finney . . . poor dude . . . Babylon, didn't you tell her about Finney . . . his . . . uh, condition?"

He's rattled, and I cannot help but objectively report that he is cute when he's rattled. "I did, Gabe, I swear I did," I tell him. "But she'd already set her sights on another guy. . . ." Hmm, this is harder to express than I thought. "You," I say quietly.

"Who?"

I turn up the volume. "You, Gabe. You. Tabby likes you."

His face becomes so hard to read it might as well be Sanskrit. "Me?" he says. "Well, that's almost funny." His face shifts into something mischievous. "You know what that means, don't you?"

Nope, haven't got a clue. All I know is I feel his look pour over me, too warm and too intimate for a sunny day in a very public place.

"What we've got here, mathematically speaking," he says, "is a rhombus."

"Rhombus?" Damn, I hate math.

"A four-sided figure," he explains.

Which means . . .

"Babyl? Babylon? I need you!" Emmalee nearly knocks Finney over opening the motor home door; out pops her head, her plea.

If only I wasn't stuck to the spot like some wax museum display.

"Babyl?"

Hearing my name again breaks the spell. "Got to go," I tell Gabe, and hurry after Emmalee. I can't remember when I was so glad to see a safety pin! If only there was one to hold the pieces of my life in place.

The day whizzes by. Eventually Nae-Jo catches up to us, and Emmalee finds plenty for her to do too. We hustle nonstop, six different setups all over the beach and amusement park, but keeping busy can't fully steer my mind clear of Gabe.

After all, he's only a few feet away — I can hear him laughing, watch him working in the sun. I've connected the dots, all right: Finney likes Tabby, Tabby likes Gabe . . . and Gabe likes me. He *likes* me. As in, "that way."

What am I thinking? No, what am I feeling? Something? Anything?

"So who's ready for some rides?"

By eight P.M., we wrap our last shot, and I for one wouldn't mind being carried out of Coney on a stretcher. Who has the energy for rides? Gabe, apparently. He's put the question to Tabby, Nae-Jo, and me, Finney lurking behind him, Paulina and Emmalee sending off our models and crew. I've managed to avoid Gabe's eyes since he dropped his geometric reference, and I do my best to continue looking elsewhere, *anywhere* elsewhere.

"Sounds good," says Nae-Jo, who I could murder right about now.

"Nae, you must have sunstroke," I grumble. "I'm spent!"

Tabby squints at me. "Yes, Babylon, you do look half dead!" she says. I so appreciate the compliment. "You ought to head back, take a nice shower, you'll feel better." She bats her eyes — yes, literally, bats them — at Gabe. "I'd love to go on some rides, Gabe. I'm not tired at all."

Gabe pretends not to hear her. "Come on, Babylon — what's the difference between sitting on the D train and sitting on the Cyclone?" All straight-faced and rational, he coerces me with logic. "Except you get to scream your head off, and I can't think of a better way to unwind after a long, hard day."

Here come Paulina and Emmalee — to my rescue, I hope.

"Hey, check it out!" Paulina flashes a fat roll of what looks like cardboard ribbon. Tickets. "Just a little Coney Island swag."

Sometimes life is like a ride — you get urged on and swept up, and before you can even strap in tight, you're dizzy. That's how I feel boarding the legendarily rickety wooden coaster. But I skip out of sharing a seat with Gabe; it's him crammed in with Tabby and Finney in front of Emmalee and me — Paulina and Nae-Jo grabbing the last car for maximum fear factor.

Slowly, slowly, with a creaky chug, the carts begin their ascent up that first and most terrifying hill. "Em," I say, "guess who pretty much told me flat out he wants to get with me?"

"I don't have to guess — I already know." She links her arm through mine, fingers clutching as we continue our virtually vertical climb. "Oh, this is a bad idea. . . ."

"I know! It's a terrible idea! Me . . . and Gabe? Now? With everything that's going on?"

"I'm talking about this ride, not Gabe!" she says, her pitch peaking, her grasp tightening. "Please, Babyl, if I didn't think he was a good guy I would have said something ages ago. I like him. He's cool and smart — smart-assy — but nice, sort of like you. Anyway, the question isn't what I think of Gabe." She gulps at the thinning atmosphere. "The question is: What do *you* think of Gabe?"

My answer? A very long, very loud, very out-of-control shriek as we plummet to the bottom that rushes up to meet us yet never seems to come.

And so the night progresses. Hot dogs and ripple fries at the original Nathan's. Bumper cars, cotton candy, "Shoot the Freak." I just go with it — I'm on the ride. Gabe seems content to fire squirt guns at clown faces and smother his frank with relish and act like nothing's up, all the while observing me from the sides of his eyes. And somehow, strangely, I become accustomed to his subtle yet persistent scrutiny; I start to check for his gaze, and finding it on me, feel a flush and a heat and a pride, as if I've just won an award for doing absolutely nothing but being myself.

Paulina flirts with some rockabilly guys in front of a bar, while Nae-Jo does handstands on the boardwalk. Barkers throw their lines at Emmalee, who laughs them off without a care. Tabby bops around giddily, eating a soft-serve ice-cream cone in a borderline obscene manner she must have read about in *Cosmo*. These are people I know, surrounded by people I don't know — a huge throng of Friday night summertime revelers — yet it's all unreal, indistinct, trippily irrelevant. Everything just seems to orbit around me.

Then we're at the Wonder Wheel, that fabled Ferris wheel, the final ride, and somehow it's me and Gabe alone in a swinging cage — the cage big enough for four, for six, yet just for us. The cage is blue and the night is black and I can see the city below spanning in all directions. I look at the city. Gabe looks at me.

"This was so worth waiting for," he says evenly.

My eyes memorize the great array of earthly lights as I say, "Oh? You've been waiting long?"

"What day did you start at *Orange*?" His voice sounds thick, like something I could carve.

I look at him now, and he takes my gaze like I've offered him a chalice. Probably I should say something, something that starts with, "You know, Gabe . . ." Something full of where I'm ats and who I ams, excuses and explanations. But I don't. All I do is let him look at me, full-on now, close up now.

"You know, Babylon, there's going to be fireworks. . . ."

As soon as he says it they start, out on the beach, starbursts and pinwheels and skyrockets, pink and green and white. We watch for a while, as we travel around and around, going absolutely nowhere in space, and then stop on the top — let 'em off, let 'em on.

That's when Gabe says it again, whispers it, really.

"Babylon, there's going to be fireworks. . . ." And at first I'm confused, since starbursts and pinwheels and skyrockets are already sparking the darkness. But then, of course, I know what he means. I know exactly what he means, the instant he places his lips against mine.

DOES EVERYONE REALLY HATE YOU?

Are you A) an evil traitor who deserves the social equivalent of the death penalty, B) unjustly accused and completely innocent, or C) just a little paranoid?

The *Orange* office is all abuzz. First thing Monday morning, Izzie announces Berni O'Rourke's big promotion from Amuse! to Exec! Editor. Berni makes a speech in her keening squeak about what an honor it will be to serve as Izzie's second-in-command, and how pleased she is that it all came down while the Readers Run Amok program is in full swing. It's all boring office politics to me, but I join in when everybody whoops and applauds, converging on Berni to sprinkle the figurative confetti of congrats.

I'm simply glad to let my smile out, having spent the weekend biting my lip to keep it from spreading across my face. Because clearly what went down on the Wonder Wheel Friday night — that single, head-spinning, experimental but not at all tentative smooch — is not for public disclosure, at least not till I get a grip on what the hell it means. Believe it or not, I didn't even tell Emmalee. So there was no hand-holding when we got off the ride, no snuggling on the subway, and certainly no Gabe in the Dorm of Doom. Just a wistful, "See you, Babyl," and a soft, "Later, Gabe" as we went our separate ways.

Not that I didn't relive and ruminate on the kiss all week-end. Was it simply one amazing moment up in the air against a backdrop of light-spattered sky? Or the prelude to some-thing more? All I know is Gabe made his point, as profoundly as he could with any poem, and is no doubt waiting for me to make the next move. Whenever I tried to figure out what that might be, a floating image of a furious Tabby arose, ren-dering me useless.

So I'm glad to get back to work this morning — except as soon as I walk into my office after the announcement I'm confronted by another freaked-out female, and this one's not a figment of my imagination. Natalie's on the phone, and I scarcely recognize my normally laid-back, good-natured mentor.

"She's such a *bitch*!" Natalie fumes while motioning for me to come in and shut the door. "After all those promises she made!" She pauses, sniffles. "I mean, Berni O'Rourke?! Who knew anything that huge could get that far up some-one's ass! Which is the sole reason she got the gig; she's completely unqualified! I wouldn't trust the woman to address an envelope, much less edit an article!"

Natalie's quiet once more, heeding the other end of the line. "Well," she says, with a bitter laugh, "first I need to scrounge up a Valium, or at least some chamomile tea. Anything to keep me from going medieval in the corner office."

She hangs up, then stares at me, face about to crumble. I can tell she's aching and I don't know what to do — till I remember the stash in my purse. I pull out the Coney Island saltwater taffy and Natalie attacks it. She doesn't go into details — with her teeth gnashing the sticky candy, enunciation is problematic — but she doesn't need to. A lobotomized bunny could ascertain that she deems Izzie's decision the ultimate betrayal.

Tabby, on the other hand, couldn't be more thrilled. "Well, you all know Berni adores me," she gloats that evening in the suite, "so now that she's Izzie's second-in-command, I'll be a shoo-in for the column. Sorry!"

Maybe so. Nepotism is a potent force. But if Tabby's dreams of *Orange* glory are about to come to fruition, a few days later her fantasy of a personal life falls apart.

There I am, innocently placing an order at the pizzeria — takeout for me and Natalie, who's been drowning her sorrows in cheese — when Gabe appears behind me in line.

"Geez, Babylon, you must be hungry!" he says, nodding as the pizza guy loads half a pie and a spinach calzone into the oven.

It's the first I've seen of him since Coney Island, and it makes my heart leap. "Surely you didn't mistake me for one of those I'll-just-have-a-salad girls?" I say, keeping it casual. I don't mention that most of the food is for Nat.

"When it comes to you, Babylon, I don't make presumptions." He orders a meatball hero. "So how've you been?"

"Oh, I'm good," I say, my glance darting, then circling back to rest on his.

"Good. I'm glad you're good," he says. "In case you haven't noticed, I've got a vested interest in your welfare." His fingers gravitate toward mine, our touch electric. Then I move away, slip into a booth. Gabe sits across from me.

"You think it's an accident I'm here?" he asks. "Not that I'm stalking you or anything; I just happened to notice you've been picking up lunch here the last couple of days, so . . . look, I really wanted to call you, drop by your office or something, but I didn't —"

"Gabe — me too, but it's like this —"

"The Tabby thing, I know, but —"

"No, yes, not just that, I —"

Will either of us complete a sentence in this lifetime? Yes. Him. He seizes my hand, which shuts me up.

"You're a good person, Babylon, you don't want to get

184

involved with me because you don't want to hurt your friend," he says. "I respect that, I do. But you know I like you, and I know you like me."

Okay. He said it. Let his words back up his action. That's crucial. Because sometimes a boy will kiss you to check off any of a million possibilities on an unseen agenda. Not this boy, though. This boy is straight up.

"You *do* like me, right? I'm not delusional, right?"

No, not delusional. Adorable, but not delusional. "Yes, Gabe, I like you." Still, I free my hand to fiddle with canisters of oregano, pepper, garlic. "But it's complicated."

"No, it's simple," he says. "Look, I didn't want to kiss you and then let the chips fall where they may. That kiss means something to me, and . . . I want another one, I want a whole series, in rapid succession."

I muse for a second on how nice that would be. But after everything I said to Tabby . . . impossible!

"So don't worry," he says. "I took care of it."

Guys are so like that. They think they can fix everything, as if the Y chromosome comes with its own little tool kit. And suddenly I get this sting, like a mosquito bite on the brain. "Um, took care of what?"

He smiley-snarks me. "The Tabby thing."

"Gabe! You didn't! Did you? What did you —"

He reaches for my hand again. "I'm telling you, Babylon, it's cool," he says. "She came to my desk this morning, she had some questions about my Mansions of Happiness article, and I set her straight."

"Set her straight?" This is not good. "How, specifically, did you set her straight?"

"I told her about us," he says matter-of-factly.

I smack his hand. "Gabe! No! A) there *is* no us, not officially, and B) you had no right to talk to Tabby without first talking to me!"

"Wait a second, Babyl — no us?" He sounds a little hurt. "What do you call what happened on the Wonder Wheel?"

"I don't know, Gabe. I don't know," I say. "Up until the Wonder Wheel, I thought we were — well, I thought we were just friends."

"Friends!" He says it like "terrorists!"

"Maybe I had a mental block," I admit. "I knew, with you, I felt . . . something . . . but I'd made a commitment to myself that this summer was going to be about *Orange,* about work. Not guys. Not *you.*"

He leans back against the booth. "The best laid plans, huh?"

Please! He's quoting verse now? "Yeats?" I venture.

"Burns," he corrects me. "Robert Burns: 'The best laid plans of mice and men often go awry.' So now what?"

"Four slices and a spinach calzone?" the counterman calls out.

"Now?" I say. "Now I need to dose Natalie with mozzarella, and then I've got to deal with Tabby."

Gabe gets up, walks me to the cash register. "No, Babyl, I'm telling you. I talked to her. She's cool about us — me — you — whatever you want to call what you and me are."

"Yeah, uh-huh, cool," I say. For a Scottish bard-spouting Columbia sophomore-to-be, the boy knows absolutely nothing!

"Babylon! Thank God!" Natalie hails me, waving a Twizzler. "I'm halfway through this bag, and I don't even like licorice." The woman clearly has the metabolism of a fruit fly. I dump the pizza box on her desk. "Babyl? Where are you going?" she asks.

"I have to take care of something," I tell her. "Eat my slices if you want."

I book it down the hall to Amuse! A tribunal of four Run Amoks has assembled. "Tabby, let me explain —" I start.

The Amuse! office has a small sofa, ostensibly for the comfort of famous visitors. Right now, Tabby is seated in the center, Nae-Jo on one side, and Emmalee on the other, Paulina slouched against the arm. Paulina's the first to "greet" me.

"You here to stick the knife in a little deeper, Babylon?" she says.

I could appreciate her standing up for Tabby, if there wasn't an icy glint of malice in her small, hard eyes. "Paulina, I didn't come to talk to you," I say. "I came to talk to Tabby."

"Yeah?" Nae-Jo stands up to wag a finger in my face. "Well, maybe she does not want to be talking to you. Maybe this office is a traitor-free zone, Babylon."

Hardest of all is Emmalee, who doesn't say a thing. Could be she changed her mind about me and Gabe going for it. Or she's angry that I didn't confide in her about the kiss. I don't know what she's thinking — her lashes hide what's inside.

"I can fight my own battles, thank you, Nae-Jo," Tabby says. She has been crying, but she's not crying anymore. Now she is quivering with indignation. "But I am not going to fight. I wouldn't lower myself."

I feel for her, I do — she has a right to be upset. So I prep for a verbal attack — a monologue stolen from a soap opera.

"It's quite obvious that you knew from the get-go you didn't have the stuff to make it here," Tabby says. "I mean, remember when you first tried to speak in front of the senior staff? It was laughable, Izzie had to cut you off — she didn't want you to embarrass yourself. And your 'Girls Helping Girls' concept is pitifully lame. All you've got is a bunch of kids with cheapo crappy cameras! How professional!

"So, really, Babylon it's no surprise that you would fool

around with the first boy who pays you any mind whatso-ever, even though you knew another girl — one of your ha-ha friends — liked him. Well, you and Gabe deserve each other, as far as I'm concerned. But what I don't understand, what I simply cannot fathom, is why you bothered to shovel all that bull-poop about unity and harmony that none of us believed for a second anyway.

"And now here you are with some big apology or expla-nation or something? Don't bother. I don't think any of us want to hear it, and I personally have to leave for an appoint-ment at MTV. Yes, mm-hmm, Izzie's taping a segment for their new show *Charisma,* and she wants me at her side."

With that, she squares her shoulders, tosses her moun-tainous hair, and exits, stage left.

Current population, New York City: Roughly eight mil-lion. Current temperature: Hovering around one hundred. Current number of amigas available for me to beat the heat with: Zero. You got it: NYC plunges headlong into a heat wave just in time for me to get the freeze routine from the Run Amoks. It's the day after Tabby's tirade, and they all blew off work at noon to traipse off to an East Hampton pool party hosted by some rapper-turned-record label mogul. Technically, I'm invited — it's an unwritten Run Amok rule that if one of us gets an E ticket, the rest of us are plus-one, -two, -three, and -four. But I am not exactly feeling the love from my so-called girls, so why go? To jockey for position over a platter of chilled shrimp? No thank you.

My alternate activity: a whole lot of nothing. No, I'm not seeing Gabe. He e-mailed me to find out if I undid his damage with Tabby — and I hit him back to report that Run Amok rapport repair was still under construction. I'm just not ready to see him yet. Correction: Parts of me are ready, willing, and eager to see him, other parts are not, and because my heart, mind, body, and soul travel as a total package, there is no Gabe in my immediate future.

Besides, I've got my period, and all the associated sebaceous gland activity that goes with it. And if that's not enough to dampen my disposition, I got a look at preliminary designs for "Girls Helping Girls," and they . . . well, they don't exactly suck, but I'm not jumping for joy either. Maybe if Tabby hadn't dissed the Think! pages I'd be more into Paulina's layouts. I'm not even feeling my juice enough to work on my "Girls vs. Girls" outline, and it's not near done yet.

Damn. I'm sweaty. And crampy. And zitty. And depressed. And alone. All I want to do is wallow.

By the time the Run Amoks return from the Hamptons, I am no longer scorned as devil spawn. Apparently the host went overboard on the guest list while skimping on the shrimp, and there's nothing worse than hungry, disgruntled celebs. Plus, due to extreme heat there was a power outage on the Long

Island Railroad, imprisoning Em, Tabby, Paulina, and Nae in an un-air-conditioned train car for about an hour. The old Dorm of Doom must have seemed like bliss by comparison.

The first person to break the silent treatment is Emmalee, who sits on a stool in the kitchenette, watching me whip up a smoothie. Banana, yogurt, ice cubes, whirred with a whiff of vanilla extract — a Babylon special.

"Can I please tell you about my last eleven hours of torment?" she asks.

"Sure — if you no longer equate me with Damien's sister."

Emmalee winces. "Sorry, Babyl — but you could have told me something happened between you and Gabe. I can't believe you kept it to yourself, when I tell you everything."

"I know; you're right. I was going to . . ." I trail off, then come back at her. "Still, you basically gave Gabe and me your blessing, but you didn't stand up for me when Tabby chewed me out."

"Babyl, you know I support you. I just didn't think it was my place to say anything."

She's right about that — this is between me and Tabby.

Paulina corners us, eyes my frothy concoction. "Can I get some of that?" she asks.

Why not? I share, pouring some for Em as well.

"You guys talking about Tabby? Man, she sure went off on you yesterday." Paulina comments over a smoothie moustache.

"Yeah, well, I'm not about to defend myself, to her or to you, Paulina, because I committed no crime!" I'm serious, but I keep my voice low. "I didn't go for Gabe — not intentionally anyway — and if Tabby thinks I 'stole' him she needs a twelve-step program to get off those hallucinogens."

Paulina smirks. "She'd better settle for Finney if she wants to see any action this summer," she says. "I'm all for aiming high as far as guys are concerned, but Tabby has no concept when it comes to who's in and who's out of her league."

"You don't have to whisper — she's snoring like a bulldog," Nae-Jo informs us, helping herself to a swig from Paulina's glass. "Couldn't even get her to brush her teeth before she passed out in there."

Paulina rolls her eyes. "That one's developing a prinking droblem."

I laugh. "Look who's talking."

"Hey, I can handle my liquor," she insists, and except for the slip-and-fall sangria incident, I guess I'd have to agree. Paulina knows her limits — she likes to test them, but she knows them. "Besides, Tabby uses alcohol for liquid courage." She glances around for corroboration. "Am I right?"

Nae-Jo inclines her head. "I hate to say it, I love my roomie, but you do not want to get her drunk. You should have seen her today; it was em-bar-ass-ing!"

I look at Emmalee — who literally blushes. "Babylon,

she was flashing!" Em admits. "Everyone from waiters to Wentworth Miller!"

"Whoa, Wentworth Miller was there?" I say. "That boy is hot!"

From there the convo segues on to the trivial subject of celebrities in bathing suits. But that's cool — I've already made a decision. Seems to me that Tabby is starved for attention, and come tomorrow morning I'm going to give her some — whether she likes it or not.

HOW TO TELL IF HE'S A DIAMOND IN THE ROUGH

Sometimes chemistry takes a minute to kick in, so don't be so quick to judge a boy. He may just be a valiant knight in shabby armor . . . or a rock star in disguise. . . .

All's quiet in the Dorm of Doom, with three Run Amoks already braving rush hour on their way to work and one still ensconced in her room. Me, I'm dressed and ready to go — but I guess I can be late for once. I know I won't get anything accomplished till I have it out with Tabby once and for all.

First, I try tapping on her door; then I knock. To no avail. So I just go in. If noise doesn't rouse her, the aroma rising from the container of high-octane coffee I've picked up from Starbucks is bound to. "Ta-a-a-a-by," I say gently to the mound under the covers. "Oh, Ta-a-a-a-aby!"

The mound makes a muffled sound. I sit on the floor beside the bed until I detect a slight motion from the mound.

"Come on, Tabby, wake up," I say.

Slowly, hair emerges, then more hair, then, finally, her face. "Babyluggh?" she croaks.

"That's right," I say. "I come bearing the magic elixir of friendship, also known as grande mochaccino."

Her head lifts painfully, then plops back on the pillow; Tabby stares at the ceiling. She's not going to make this easy for me. "Look, I just want to tell you that I'm sorry about the whole thing with Gabe but I really, truly wasn't trying to screw you over."

I wonder how long she'll let my words hang in the air. Eventually Tabby pushes up her pillows, leans against them, and reaches for my steaming peace offering. She takes a sip, sighs, and emits another ugh.

"I mean it, Tabby," I say. "I never wanted you to get hurt. You have to believe that."

"Oh, Babyl," she says, "I do. I'm not a fool. I guess I was just trying to put it on you so I wouldn't have to accept the plain simple fact that when it comes to guys, I'm just a big loser. I mean, if it wasn't you who got Gabe it would've been Emmalee or Nae-Jo, or Paulina would have plowed through him in three days flat. But it wouldn't have been me. And it's so not fair! I try so hard to get guys to like me and they never do!"

"Well, maybe that's just it," I tell her. "Trying *so* hard

tends to come across as trying *too* hard. It's when you're not trying at all, when you're just being you, that guys take notice."

"Easy for you to say."

"Easy for you too. And you know who I'm talking about."

She's quiet for a moment. Then she says, "Finney."

"Yes, Finney. You didn't give him the time of day, but he's been entranced by you from the minute we got to Kult Ink, because what he saw was this cool, strong, confident girl who has the world on a string."

She focuses on me for the first time. "Is that how you see me?" she asks directly.

"Tabby, of course! You're a Run Amok! You beat out thousands of girls to become Amuse! Editor of *Orange,* and look at the amazing section you've put together for our issue."

"Well, I do have a way about me." Smiling, she struggles to sit up taller in bed but slumps back down, mochaccino sloshing. "Although today it feels like my way has gone astray. You think I could call in sick?"

"Forget it, Tabby! Since Berni's been promoted, you *are* the Amuse! department. So I suggest you get your butt in the shower." Standing up, I take the coffee container from her. "And make it snappy. I'll wait for you."

A thrashing of the covers, a fumble for flip-flops, and

she's out of bed and down the hall. "Ooh, Babyl?" She pauses at the bathroom door, "I was just wondering — what do *you* think of Finney?"

"I think he's whip smart and seriously sweet," I say. "Maybe not as cool as you, but he definitely has potential."

Even E-i-Cs get a vacation. Izzie's off on hers, down in Brazil with her soccer player. Her absence sends the office into a state of semi-stupor, everyone chilling while the cat's away. That's why I wasn't too concerned about coming in late. And why I have no qualms about strolling over to the *Squawk* side of the floor, scoping out Gabe's desk amid the boys' club maze of cubicles, and saying, "Hey! I just came by to say hey! So: Hey!"

He swivels away from his computer and studies me. "You didn't change your hair again," he says. "But something's got you looking like you just invented oxygen."

"Let's just say me and a certain Run Amok have come to terms."

Gabe processes this and gives me a huge grin. "That's great!" he says. "So how about lending me some of that *Orange* juice, Babyl, because I've got real writer's block. They gave me another obit to write for *Squawk,* which is paramount . . . except, of course, that somebody did die. . . . You ever hear of Violet Garvey? Famously unfamous female blues guitarist? Bonnie Raitt, Sheryl Crow, they all owe her this enormous debt. She was a leader, a legend, the one and only. I don't even know where to start!"

I beam at him, knowing his chops better than he does. "Sounds to me like you just wrote it," I say. "What you told me, Gabe, it's so honest, so direct. Quit looking for the quintessential metaphor or turn of phrase and put it down straight from the heart."

He gets it then, turns to his computer, types a few words, turns back to me. "Babylon Edison, you are a goddess!"

"Ah, well," I shrug, all nonchalant, and leave him with a "later!"

Gabe pummels his keyboard, and I go on to another encounter — this one taking place in that most essential of venues, the ladies' room. I do my business, come out to wash up, and check myself in the mirror. Leisurely. I do not scurry off just because the Infernal Intern, better known as Matumba, is on my left. I simply smile at her.

"Babylon, hey," she says. "How's it going?"

Hmm, no evil in her tone. Is she actually being pleasant? "Really great," I say. "This summer is turning out to be everything I hoped for, and more."

"That's cool," says Matumba. "Because New York's not for everyone. My first year up from Virginia? Took me a month before I could swipe my MetroCard correctly."

Okay, does she think I have early-onset Alzheimer's?

That the way she's been treating the Run Amoks from our first day isn't etched on my memory? I put these thoughts onto my face where she can read them, but then I let it go — bygones being bygones and blah-blah-blah. Matumba looks relieved that I don't drag her over the coals.

"So, you told your girl Tabby to give me an assignment?" she asks.

"Oh? Tabby gave me credit for something?" Astonishing!

Matumba sucks her teeth. "Well, when she came up to me and asked me if I could do something for her, I *may* have shown her a little attitude. She threw your name out right quick after that."

I nod. "Sounds like Tabby."

"Anyway, I got to interview Mandolyn Rollins. They say she's the next Christina Ricci. Plus, it'll be my first byline."

That's an eyebrow-raiser. "You've been interning here forever, and you've never written anything?"

Matumba purses her lips. "Not exactly forever, but I've been taking care of Izzie from the start, and that's . . . let's just say I'm busy."

This is weird to me. Even though Kult Ink relies on interns for assistant duties, I figured Izzie would have encouraged Matumba to be more than her calendar-keeper and telephone monitor.

"Anyway . . ." Matumba runs a finger along her eyebrows, smoothing them. "I like your natural. I've been relaxing my hair so long it'll probably fall out before I graduate."

I can't quite commiserate — I never went in for chemicals. "Well, it's not like it's no-maintenance, but thanks," I say. "Emmalee did it."

Matumba bugs her eyes. "You're lying! Goldilocks knows how to do black hair?"

It's always annoying when people make race-based presumptions, but the truth is I was taken aback myself — black hair is, what can I say, a black thing. So I laugh. "Guess she's a savant or something. But I'm sure she'd be glad to give you a consultation." Then I add, "If you're nice, that is."

Enough of my slacking and socializing! The other Run Amoks can take it easy. Now that all the text has been merged with Paulina's layouts, it's up to the copy department to do its thing, making sure we're all factually and grammatically correct. But I've still got to hustle on "Girls vs. Girls." My research is complete, but I'm not quite finished finessing the outline for Izzie's perusal. My intention is to present it to her at the meeting next week where she'll see our page proofs for the first time. It's going to blow her away! Plus, it's so detailed I'll be able to turn in a finished manuscript pretty easily. Paulina will have to put in some overtime to design it — and the copy editors might get mad — but we'll be able to get it into the Run Amok issue if Izzie sanctions it. And she will, I just know it.

Only — ouch! — the tension of my workload is killing my neck and shoulders. Lucky me, right around quitting time, the queen bee of glamour swag dings my in-box:

e.roberts: marguerite just gave me invites to an event at a new spa! what would you say to a spa mani-pedi and massage?

b.edison: i'd say: helllloooo, mani-pedi and massage! sign me up!

We head out to Ta-Da! Spa on the Upper East Side for a pamper party.

"So, after this, it's off to Anti-Matter, right?" I ask as we luxuriate side by side, one foot apiece in a tub full of suds, the other pumiced soothingly by silent aestheticians.

"Yes, it'll be nice, going out with a big group," Em replies. "Although we'll all feel like extras in a romantic comedy called *Gabe and Babyl's First Date*," she can't resist adding.

"Mmmm," I murmur as my left foot nudges the third ring of ecstasy. Anti-Matter, this new club on the Lower East Side, is acquiring a rep for its Free Form Forum — an open mike with a twist. There's music, sure, but also comedy, spoken word, magic, whatev. An anything-goes entertainment adventure. A Kult Ink crowd. The fact that Gabe's going, that's simply a bonus.

We all meet up and commandeer tables up front, Gabe and I sitting side by side. "Listen," he says, leaning in to me, "no matter how weird the acts get, you have to promise you'll stay till the special surprise guest."

I'm so mellow from the ministrations I received at Ta-Da! Spa a few hours ago, he could have insisted I stay for the vivisection and I would have said okay.

"Hey, I'm Dudeman, you can call me Dudeman," says a laconic parenthesis of a person in a porkpie hat from the small stage up front. "Welcome to the Free Form Forum. I am your humble servant and master of ceremonies. Before we begin I must remind you discriminating patrons of pop culture that tonight's performers are not paid, so when the Lute of Tips gets passed around, tip well, tip hard, and tip often — just don't tip over."

With that, the eclectic lineup begins, each solo, duo, or group getting exactly seven minutes to charm us. Some acts are funny, some are sweet, some are really out-there, and some are just plain awful, but we're having such a blast it's all good. Nae-Jo arm wrestles a guy from *Plank*; Paulina canoodles with her latest love interest, an associate editor at *RoundBox* who must be pushing twenty-five; Matumba, Emmalee, and I discuss fall fashion (a subject I have a newfound appreciation for) — which trends are hit and which are dis. Tabby actually speaks to Finney — just casually, she's simply being nice — but I think it makes him nervous. He keeps leaping up and disappearing for minutes at a time, like he's got the proverbial ants in his pants.

"Last up, my fine-feathered aficionados, is a talented young ivory-tickler," says Dudeman. "And bear in mind that when you tip after this act, your tips also go to me and my able-bodied assistant, our soundman Marco, who will now help me push the almighty eighty-eights to center stage." Dudeman and Marco make a production of heaving a piano on wheels into place, just as I feel Gabe give me a squeeze above the knee that makes me leap in my seat.

"This is it," he says excitedly.

"Ladies and gents," says Dudeman, "please welcome the unflappable, inimitable, and occasionally erroneous Finney!"

Finney? As in *our* Finney!? Apparently! And when did he slip into that tuxedo jacket, complete with long tails? He bounds for the stage and, with a flourish, casts aside the bench, then launches his attack. *Tickling* the ivories?! He lambastes them, rocking and rolling, really fast and rhythmic, sweeping just about every single one of those eighty-eight keys. His fingers fly, his feet stomp, his smile engulfs his elfin face, and his hair flops around madly. If he had stage fright before, there's no sign of it now — the boy is a maestro, and he knows it. Us? We had no clue. Except Gabe, who's banging the table and hollering, exhorting Finney to new percussive heights. There's a monumental crescendo — then a ruckus of applause.

Finney turns toward the crowd with a wicked grin, flips his forelock, and boogie-woogies into another number, this one with lyrics that seem somehow familiar: "You . . . leave me . . . breathless . . . AHHHH!" The full-of-surprises Finney sings, too, and when I can tear my eyes off the inferno onstage — doing what in its own wild way is a love song — I steal a look at Tabby, but she's turned her chair around, her back to me. All I see is that corona of frizz.

Now Finney speaks: "That was 'Breathless,' by the Killer himself, Jerry Lee Lewis. Now, before Dudeman gets out his hook, I'd like to do an original."

Finney finds the bench, sits down, and begins to play a ballad. Purging the wacky in favor of the deep and soulful, the sincere and bittersweet, he croons:

"If I were Rubens and you were my muse
I'd render your beauty in a million subtle hues.
If I were Rubens and you sat for me
The light that fell around you would be heavenly.
If I were Rubens I'd live to serve
Every noble ounce of every dimple, slope, and curve.
If I were Rubens I would turn to art
The emotions your presence stirs in my heart.

But I'm no Rubens, can't even draw a line
Much less a beauty, great and sure and fine.
No, I am no Rubens, and all I draw is scorn
From the beauty oblivious to the day I was born."

Oh my God! Right around the last line I realize whom the song is about. And as Tabby floats up from her seat, I'm about to burst with happiness — because she realizes it too.

"I WAS PROFILED!"

What could be worse than finding out, first-hand, that not everyone understands all girls are created equal? Discovering that you've been wrongly judged by the person you respect the most . . .

So much for my human-nature assessment skills. I would've expected Tabby in love to be a more room-filling, energy-sucking version of Tabby not in love. But no. Her final über-boisterous moment was to rush the Anti-Matter stage and fall into Finney's arms as the crowd roared. Ever since, she's gone from blunt instrument to cumulous cloud, her braying outbursts replaced by soft sighs. It's had a calming effect on the Dorm of Doom, bringing the vibe down a notch or twelve.

Around the office, things are silky smooth too. Izzie's back from hiatus, but her focus is elsewhere — according to my new best friend Matumba, she's in negotiations with Chick-TV for her own show, *Izzie Does It*. Most of the day-to-day operations have shifted to Berni, who's taking the job seriously, flinging orders with a dictator's zeal. We'd all probably be uptight if she didn't come off like Cartman demanding we respect his uh-thor-uh-tie.

It took practically the whole summer, but here we Run Amoks are, settled into a real New York groove, our flow in sync with the humongous humming force of the city. The only thing making us a little jumpy is our upcoming final meeting as *Orange* editors, when Izzie will critique our page proofs and make her tweaks. Hopefully, they'll be minor — a sidebar here, a photo there. Still, there's a chance she could hate everything, tear our stuff to smithereens — that would mean making revisions at warp speed.

Fortunately for me, I've got backup. I'll present "Girls Helping Girls" and my outline for "Girls vs. Girls" simultaneously. In a perfect world, Izzie will opt to run both stories — "G vs. G" for the Run Amok issue and "Helping" in an upcoming *Orange.* Or she may even elect to devote extra pages to Think! and run both stories side by side. Even if she only chooses one — even if it's the one I'm less enthused about — she'll see how motivated and determined I am, what an intrepid reporter. And, basically, that's my bid for the column. I may not get it, but I'm proud that I approached the competition with integrity. I didn't have to die my hair or ink my skin to impress Izzie LaPointe.

So when Emmalee tries to lure me into an extended back-to-school shopping spree, my answer is, "No."

"Goodness, Babylon," she says. "Your page proofs are

done; even your captions are literary. Come on — I've got the coordinates for a sample sale."

Visions of discounted designer gear dance in my head but, with effort, I purge them. "Need I remind you that 'Girls vs. Girls' is still in a state of flux?" I say.

"Oh," she responds. "That."

It seems like Em wants to say more. Does she think presenting "Girls vs. Girls" is a bad idea? Could she be jealous that I have this extra edge? I don't push her to speak. "Look, make like my personal shopper and scout some stuff for me," I say instead. "Then once I'm satisfied I've got the Pulitzer on lock I'll focus on the frivolities of fashion."

Emmalee makes a face at the last part of my remark, but she knows I'm teasing — my sense of style has blossomed, largely due to her tutelage. "All right," she says. "But let's do something low-key later . . . just us." She pauses. The air between us is fraught with a subject we don't dare mention yet grows more ominous every day — the fact that it's the third week in August, that we only have one more week together, that Houston and Boston might as well be light-years away from each other.

Holding on to Emmalee's gaze, knowing exactly what she's feeling, I flash on all we've meant to each other these last two months. "Definitely," I tell her.

Off she goes to battle fashionistas from Fifth Avenue to

SoHo while I go back to my outline. But I'm quick to respond to a sharp rapping on the doorjamb.

"Matumba?" I say. She looks perturbed. "You okay?"

"This place is a ghost town — nobody's here!" she says. "And I am really in a bind, Babylon. I was talking to this cutie in McDonald's on my lunch break, and I must have gone blonde for a minute — I forgot to pick up Izzie's dry cleaning."

My mind grapples with these two unbelievable bits of data — that Matumba deigns to dine at Mickey D's, and that part of her job description includes the ferrying of cellophane-enclosed clothing.

"It'll take five minutes, ten tops," she rushes on, undeterred by my puzzled expression. "All you have to do is sit at my desk, cover the phones . . ."

Phones? I want to tell her, "I don't *do* phones," which is the truth — I have no idea how to transfer a call. But she looks desperate, and I cave.

"Babyl, I so owe you!" Matumba says. "She's in there with Berni and Marguerite, deliberating outfits for the MTV Movie Awards. They won't even notice I'm AWOL."

"Okay, Matumba, but A) you better get back in a hurry and B) damn right you owe me," I tell her, then walk down the hall and sit gingerly at her desk outside the E-i-C's domain. I can hear Izzie and her lieutenants chatting away; the door's ajar. Holding my breath, I lean over for a peep. It's like a Creamsicle in there! Off-white walls and milky glass, with sofa, shag rug, and lampshades in a succulent shade of guess what. There's even a potted plant bearing tiny oranges. A rolling rack stands in the middle of the room, groaning with dresses, skirts, and tops from Izzie's favorite designers. Emmalee told me once that E-i-Cs often borrow stuff for TV appearances and special events.

Whisking briskly through the hangers, Izzie withdraws a scoop-neck silvery sheath with a handkerchief hem. "Ooh, this is cute!" she cries, holding it against her body.

A thought occurs to me: Make a noise, alert her to your presence — here's Babylon, pitching in, helping out. So what if it gets Matumba in trouble as long as Izzie knows what kind of girl you are. Then, horrified for allowing the notion to invade my cerebrum, I shudder inwardly. I am *not* the kind of girl who'd screw someone to get ahead; I'm just not. Carefully, quietly, I swivel away.

"That would look fabulous on you!" comes Berni's trade-mark squeal.

"It would show off your tan and your figure, and it's so LA," adds Marguerite.

Sycophants in stereo! I think, but Izzie's accustomed to it. "Uch, did I tell you they may want to shoot *Izzie Does It* in LA?" she gripes. "Can you imagine the jet lag of bicoastal commuting?"

"Oh, but Izzie! Your own show. I still can't believe it," says Berni.

"Why not?" Izzie's like a puma, pouncing on the slightest negativity. "I am so ready for the next level," she asserts.

"Oh, oh, of course!" Berni says. "I just mean I can't believe those obtuse Chick-TV producers finally came to their senses."

I shouldn't be eavesdropping, but what else can I do? Cybersurfing's off-limits since I don't know Matumba's password. So I zone out, daydreaming that I'm the one running the show in the inner sanctum — checking out television attire, keeping my subordinates in line. The women flit from topic to topic — Marguerite mentioning a new complexion lotion, Berni bitching about how tough it will be to hire her replacement as Amuse! Editor. Only when the conversation segues to the Run Amoks do I rivet on every single word.

"Of course, you know best, Iz — but I'm partial to Tabby," Berni volunteers. "She'd be perfect for it. I've molded her into a regular Mini-Me."

Oh God! Could they be . . . yes they are! They're talking about the column. My breath freezes in my throat.

Marguerite puts in her bid. "Well, my vote is for Emmalee," she says. "Although, who knows if she'll have time for it if she takes that contract with Delish."

Izzie makes a dismissive sound. "You guys don't get it, do you? I made my decision before the girls even got here."

Wait! *What?!*

"So enough with the silly suspense," says Marguerite. "Which one gets the gig?"

"Oh, come on, Iz! Spill — *please*?" begs Berni.

Clearly Izzie is enjoying this. "I shouldn't," she says. "It would be unethical. . . ."

Are Berni and Marguerite thinking what I'm thinking: That making the call on a contest before it even begins is the ultimate in unethical?

"But this is *us*, Izzie," Berni says. "We're your girls."

"My girls?" boss lady says querulously. "Berni, Berni, Berni, if you and Marge were really my girls you'd be able to anticipate my choice. You'd know in an instant who represents the next generation of girls with juice."

Long, long, agonizingly long pause.

"You dumb bunnies — think demographics!" Izzie thunders. "Hello! We're already solid with jock chicks and rock chicks, so giving Nae-Jo or Paulina her own page wouldn't do a damn thing for us. And Tabby? Please! She's a loose cannon; you never know what silly thing is going to pop out of her mouth. As to Emmalee, she's the girl our readers love to hate; I'd be screwing myself if I made her a columnist. . . ."

Not Nae or Paulina, not Tabby or Em. That leaves . . .

"Use your head," Izzie says. "What segment of the population is growing like mad yet in desperate need of a voice, a venue, a community? What market does *Orange* need to sink its hooks into? Wake up, ladies! Biracial girls are the next wave! So despite the fact that she hasn't got a shred of talent, Babylon Edison is the girl with the most juice."

GIRL HELPS GIRL

Sometimes you find allies where you least expect them. . . .

The world has turned to muck. No one can see it, not even me, but that doesn't make it any less real. Matumba relieves me from my post, but her thanks come through as a garbled mess. I'm struggling against the goo, sucking it into my lungs. It must take an hour to reach the realm of Think! Once there, I blink, blink, blink — trying to clear my vision. Vaguely I identify my mentor moving toward me as I grip the back of my chair, lower myself into it.

Something, possibly Natalie's hand, touches my shoulder. Her face swims over me. She's talking like she's underwater. "Bwab-bwa-bwon?" I shake my head, desperate to clear this strangling substance. She says it again — and I realize it's my name.

"What?" My reply is a dry croak.

"What do you mean *what?*" Natalie kneels in front of me, peers up, tucks a wavy wisp behind an ear. "You — that's what. Babylon, what happened?" Her voice is tense, her features pinched with concern, but she's the one, maybe the only one, who will understand.

"Please, Natalie," I implore. "Close the door."

Vocal ability — back on track. Auditory ability too: I can hear the click of the lock, the slide of papers across the desk as Natalie pushes them aside to sit. Yes, everything is lucid now, crystalline. Natalie touches my shoulder again, lightly, a dragonfly landing. I raise my eyes to hers. And I tell her everything.

"Okay, so what do you want to do about it?" Natalie asks. None of this "Oh, Babylon, I'm so sorry" or "That's so awful!" Empathy doesn't compel her to baby me. And she hardly seems surprised. Any esteem Natalie might have had for Izzie has long since eroded. So she's being no-nonsense, and I appreciate that — yet I can only answer her with a limp question of my own.

"What *can* I do?" I ask. All that occurs to me is this: Babylon Edison = Insignificant no-talent peon whose sole commendable quality is that one of her parents happens to be white and the other black; Isabel LaPointe = Omnipotent media Medusa set on world domination. It's just so hard to accept. Izzie was everything I wanted to be. A woman of the world, and of words. Not merely a top player in my chosen field, but the only female under thirty to run a national magazine with a million-and-growing circ. Throw in her knockout looks. The killer body. All the men tripping over themselves for the privilege of being her plus-one. And the real clincher — the fact that Izzie doesn't rule some stupid piece of tabloid trash or vapid style sheet, she's the chick in charge of *Orange*. It all adds up to one amazing role model.

Except it's all a lie.

Izzie built her success on encouraging girls to be the best, to look farther and go deeper, really max out our potential. If she's a fake, what does that make us — all the girls with so-called juice? Worthless. Meaningless.

But no! *Orange* may be a stepping-stone for Izzie's ambition, but the girls who read it are still awesome — brilliant, gifted, gutsy, and idealistic. Thinking about girls like that, girls like the Run Amoks, I get a brainstorm. "Natalie, I think it's time for me to tap the power of girls helping girls firsthand."

"Babylon, you are one meeting-calling mofo," Nae-Jo comments as she, not-so-fresh from the gym and the last to arrive at the Dorm of Doom, plops between Tabby and Paulina on the couch.

"You ever hear of soap?" Paulina uses a shove as punctuation.

"Chill, chica! Do capoeira for an hour, see if you don't sweat," Nae-Jo shoves back. "I *would* be in the shower right now, but Babyl said it was urgent."

"So what's the deal, Babylon?" Paulina demands.

"Yes, Babyl, please — I don't have all night," adds Tabby. "Finney and I are going to ride the Staten Island Ferry by moonlight. Isn't that romantic?"

As usual, Emmalee refrains from comment, eyeing me from one of the armchairs. So I get to it. "Okay. You guys are looking at *Orange* magazine's brand-new columnist."

Dead silence. Followed by cacophony. Jeers and protests fill the room and I just let them rain around me. Eventually they peter out, and the Run Amoks glare at me in unison. Which prompts me to be as succinct as possible: "I was filling in for Matumba today. Izzie was in her office, and I heard her tell Berni and Marguerite that she already chose me for the page."

More outbursts from everyone but the mummified Emmalee. I wait them out.

Then I say: "Not that I'll be accepting the honor. Since she didn't pick me because I'm such a great writer or anything. She picked me for one reason and one reason only: my café-au-lait, freckles-on-caramel biracial skin."

The bomb takes a few seconds to permeate Run Amok consciousness. Then: "NO!!!" Loud, strident, angry, incredulous. From, of all people, Emmalee. She hops to her feet, and she's trembling. "Izzie wouldn't . . . she couldn't . . ."

I feel her pain. So does everyone else who helped erect the pedestal Izzie LaPointe poses on. "I'm sorry, Em," I say. "Izzie was my idol too. That's why it seems inconceivable —"

"No, Babylon, don't go there, please . . . " Emmalee is stubborn.

I push past her opposition. "We don't want to think Izzie's evil because she's meant so much to us," I argue. "But now that I know what she's really like, I realize the signs were there all along. Think about it. Tabby, remember how she conned you into including Turpentine Cocktail in 'Next Big Things'?"

Tabby stamps her foot. "I *explained* that to you, Babylon. That was just business!"

"Yeah? Well, what kind of 'business' do you call the way Izzie was cozying up to their manager backstage at the show?" I say. "And, Emmalee, what about how 'Come As You Are' morphed into 'Come As Somebody Else Wants You to Be'? How much you want to bet Izzie's courting those designers to line her closets with swag? Not to mention how she's leaning on you about that modeling contract. You think there isn't something in it for Izzie, discovering a fresh new star for the Delish agency?"

"You just don't understand how things work, Babylon," pipes up Nae-Jo, suddenly an authority on the machinations of industry.

"Don't I? Here's another tidbit for you," I challenge. "Were you aware that almost all the girls featured in 'Tang!'

are linked to Izzie's network, six degrees of separation or less from the rich and influential?"

Finally I strike a nerve. "Well, not me!" avows Nae-Jo. "Nobody rich in my neighborhood, and we got a different kind of influential!" She defends herself, then whistles softly. "But if what you say is true, Babylon, that's really . . . that's messed up."

Paulina hoists herself off the couch, begins pacing the room. "I should have known!" she seethes. "That's this world for you — this friggin' species! You can't trust anyone. Izzie LaPointe, George W. Bush — what's the difference? They're all liars and phonies, and there's not a goddamn thing we can do about it."

Count on Paulina to foam up a full-on punk-rock anarchist rage. Her stormy monologue builds and builds until she abruptly stops, stricken, helpless. That's when I say: "Well, I for one refuse to let Izzie get away with it."

Paulina whirls, a familiar wicked flicker in her eyes. "Yeah? Whatever it is, I'm in," she says.

"Whoa, whoa, hold up!" Nae-Jo steps back. "So Izzie LaPointe is the chupacabra. You do what you want but I'm not about to screw up everything I busted my ass for this summer."

"Yes, be so kind as to leave me out as well!" says Tabby. "And I don't even care about the silly column anymore; my priorities have changed."

Ah, the transformative magic of first love! Still, I eye her suspiciously.

"Don't worry, Babylon, I'm not about to tell," she says. "Do as you please."

Emmalee has retreated into her cool, implacable shell. I stare her out of it. "What, exactly, do you intend to do?" she finally asks.

"Just make a point," I say. "Emmalee, you know I've been consumed by my female rivalry idea." I turn to the others. "Yeah, that's right, that was my big play. I was going to have the whole story researched and outlined so Izzie would see what a hot-shit journalist I am. Well, in light of recent discoveries, I've decided to spend the next week doing the interviews and writing it, and have *that* story appear in the Run Amok issue."

Paulina flaps her arms and huffs. "You always got to take the cerebral route, Babyl. I say we go for the viscera, like slip Izzie a massive dose of Ex-Lax or . . ."

"That's not my kind of justice," I cut her off. "And this is personal. Between Izzie and me. Anyone who wants to help — transcribe interview tapes, proofread my copy — great. You don't want to be involved, that's cool too — just stay out of my way. I'm just glad you're feeling sinister, Paulina, since you're the only person I really need to help me."

She's so hot to make trouble she can taste it. "Okay, fine, it's your show. What's my part?" she wants to know.

"Work with me," I say. "Get the photos, design the pages."

"Yeah, sure, done." She still seems a bit disappointed that no internal organs will be violated.

"And one more thing," I add. "To make sure that 'Girls vs. Girls' *has* to run, you'll need to access all the computer files for the 'Girls Helping Girls' layouts — and trash them, delete them, destroy them completely."

"I really like that thing you do," Gabe slips out an earbud to inform me.

We're encamped after hours in the Think! tank. Him: Dutifully transcribing an interview I did with a chick from an exclusive all-girls school expelled for cheating on exams. Me: Banging out the "as-told-to" account of a sixteen-year-old convicted of trying to poison her best friend — so she could get with the best friend's boyfriend. I've got four other first-persons to write for the piece, plus numerous sidebars to pull together, and Gabe's such a sweetie to spend his evenings as my assistant. Of course, he thinks the stuff I'm getting is fascinating, and besides, it's his chance to be alone with me.

"What thing?" I ask. "I have a thing?"

He bites a quadrant of his lower lip and rolls his eyes to the ceiling, then lets go. "That thing," he says. "That's what you do when you're searching for the right words."

"I don't do that!" I say dismissively.

"Yes, you do." He half rises from his chair, leans over the desk. "Usually you bite this side. . . ." Index finger (his) to lower lip (mine). I should brush him away but his touch ignites me. "But sometimes" — he trails his finger slowly from left to right — "you bite this side."

I reach my hand up to his, hold it, and plant a kiss on his fingertip. He curls his fingers around my thumb, squeezes — I can feel his intensity sure and pronounced as a pulse — and now his knuckles receive my kiss. Then I gaze into his eyes, and he into mine, and we accept this little interlude as the extent of our physical contact for now. Together we exhale as our hands release; our breath melds. We return to our respective keyboards and a few seconds later — there! I catch it: My teeth take a nibble on my left lower lip.

Totally predictable, that toiling away with Gabe would be like this — flirtation segueing into unbearable tension, then falling back to the task at hand, a wonderfully frustrating ebb and flow. It's funny — Finney and Tabby have been inseparable since the Free Form Forum, but Gabe and I are yet to have a "proper" date. That's because Gabe, he gets me — he knows I'm burning with this mission, and he supports it, so he's willing to wait till it's out of the way. Then it will be his turn. Our turn.

What I didn't know was how much of a blast it would be

working with Paulina. For three nights in a row we bust our humps on "Girls vs. Girls," eating junk food and jamming tunes — we must simultaneously shout, "I love this song!" at least half a dozen times. And she's constantly turning me on to these hilarious downloads — farting infants, mating giraffes, people doing sick things while sky-diving. The comic relief is especially welcome, because ever since I revealed my plan to the Run Amoks, Emmalee's been . . . I've been . . . she's not snubbing me . . . I'm not ignoring her . . . but there is a weirdness. Her refusal to see the truth about Izzie . . . my insistence that she do just that . . . Let's just say we've been sort of circling each other warily.

Most surprising is what a creative fireball Paulina is when she throws herself into a project. Tomorrow is the big unveiling, and she's really been cranking. No doubt this is the longest she's gone without male company since she hit puberty. Just as this occurs to me, her cell rings; she gives the caller ID a glance.

"Rhys, of course," she says.

"*Which* Rhys?" I ask. Paulina hasn't kicked her *RoundBox* Rhys to the curb quite yet, but she has met another guy — also a Brit, also named Rhys.

She shrugs. "I didn't notice. Probably young Rhys. He's such a puppy. Old Rhys, he gives me my space."

"Oh? So they're not completely interchangeable?"

That sounds judgmental, and I'd take it back if I could. "Sorry — didn't mean to be mean," I say quickly.

Paulina tosses her phone back in her purse. "Look, Babyl, I know you and the other girls — not just the Run Amoks, every other chick on the planet — I know you think I'm this massive slut, but you know what? I don't care. Maybe I'm amoral or whatever, but I just . . . I crave experience. It's not low self-esteem like half the population believes or some hormonal imbalance like the other half does. And it's not like I screw every guy I meet either, by the way — although telling you that probably blows my mega-ho image. I just want to know I can get him, whoever he is. And once I get him I take what I want — then turn him loose."

Hmm, now that she breaks it down for me it doesn't seem so outrageous. "Okay, but what about love?" I want to know.

"Not interested," she says flatly. "See, as far as I can tell there's this one essential component to love that I don't even believe exists; I think it's just a figment of mass imagination." She slaps her palm on the desk and hoots. "All right! Babyl, check it out — I think we've found our typeface!"

I peer over her shoulder, onto her computer screen, the title of the story centered on the layout.

Girls Versus Girls

"That does looks good," I say.

"It's killer!" she crows. "And get this: The font is actually called Braggadocio."

Perfect, huh? "Can I see it all caps?" I ask. "And not *versus* spelled out, just V-S-period."

GIRLS VS. GIRLS

"Yup, that's it!" I declare. "Awesome, Paulina."

She swivels and smirks at me. "Yeah, Izzie is going to lose it when she gets a load of what we've done. This is better than Ex-Lax, I got to admit."

We study the layout a bit longer, making minor changes. Paulina stretches her long arms over her head, cricks her neck this way and that. I check the clock on her computer — it's nearly midnight.

"I think we're done," I say. "Thank you so much, Paulina. I wouldn't have been able to do it without you."

"My fiendish pleasure," she says. "I can't wait to see the look on Izzie's face! I would pay good money for that."

Now that we're done, there's no turning back. I'm doing this. Tomorrow morning, at the page-proof powwow, I will officially humiliate Izzie LaPointe.

"Hey, Paulina," I say. "What we were talking about before. That thing, that love essential you don't believe in. What is it?"

Paulina turns to look at me, then back at the computer. She highlights the title, deletes it. And in its place types:

TRUST

"I BLEW IT, BIG-TIME"

What could lead a girl to give up the opportunity of a lifetime? Oh, just minor annoyances like values, integrity, and self-esteem...

Whoever said "It's always darkest before the dawn" doesn't live in the Dorm of Doom. Here, it's blazing before the dawn. Loud as hell too. There's a party going on when Paulina and I return — a small, polite, controlled one, just Nae-Jo and the *Plank* interns, back from a night game at Yankee Stadium; Emmalee, looking vaguely out of place in her own suite; Tabby and Finney; and tagalong Gabe, who brightens considerably at the sight of me. Of course Paulina, self-appointed mega-party-starter, has to call Rhys the Younger, who arrives a little past one with his band, Hugh & What Army, in tow. Their presence must bleep all the right radars, since by two A.M. it seems as though the world has converged on our dingy rooms.

No one's complaining. The summer's almost over, our work here all but complete, and sure there's an authorized Readers Run Amok closing ceremony on the schedule, but this impromptu and incendiary blowout is what we really need right now.

A beer appears in my hand, and for a nanosecond I deliberate — after all, tomorrow promises to be a day that will live in infamy. Then I think, *Yeah, so what?* Soon Gabe and I are dancing deliriously, and I notice how fully he gives himself to the music, how much freer he is than Jordan, who was always sort of stiff on the floor. By the time dawn officially breaks, revelers have slunk off like vampires except for the Kult Ink crew. We loll around in the living room, dazedly surveying the wreckage.

"Guess it's time for a shower," I murmur into Gabe's chest.

"That an invitation?" he murmurs back, lips ambulating softly from the top of my spine to the cup of my ear.

We're sitting on the floor, holding up a wall, the Manhattan Bridge coming into view through a sooty window as the early sun singes the fog. If only we were Adam and Eve, two innocents in the Garden of Eden; if only there were a waterfall a few feet away that we could run off to, then sleep together in the shade of some lush, sheltering palms. But excuse me, I'm an evolutionist, a city sprawls outside my door, and in a few hours a showdown will commence. I raise my heavy head. My eyelashes seem to be lifting dumbbells. "If only," I whisper.

Gabe rests his cheek against my brow. "Okay. I'll get Finney and those guys and we're out of here."

Yet we linger, resisting reality, paralyzed by our inter-locking limbs. Then Gabe says: "Whatever happens today, Babylon, whatever, you know, the fallout, when it's over and everything . . . ugh, I'm a blithering idiot!" He lightly slaps his own face; I still his hand.

"Don't even . . ." I say. "Just . . . don't."

"Okay," he says. "I won't . . . but I *will* see you later."

We struggle to our feet, leaning against each other. "You will," I promise.

Needles of icy water strike my flesh. The emergency genera-tor in my mind kicks on, humming and purring. I have never been more awake, more on point. I cinch the towel across my torso, calling, "Next!" as I stride out. Paulina, waiting her turn with woozy impatience, gives me a conspiratorial leer.

In our room, Emmalee's busy blow-drying her hair, head conveniently inverted. Though she wears an embroidered kimono, she sure picked out something suitable for today's main event — aka Armageddon. It's laid out on the bed. Black. Plain. Long. Straight skirt; high-necked blouse; close-toed pumps. The temperature might hit ninety by noon but she's getting her funerary finest on. Not me. I pull on white pants, a top patterned in eighties neon colors.

When Emmalee flings her head back, the expression on her face is almost one of wonder — like, what am I doing here? She parts her hair down the middle and twists it into a tight bun, schoolmarm-style.

"Where's your black veil?" I can't help asking.

Her mouth is a straight line; her nostrils slightly flared. "You think this is funny, Babylon," she says. "But I don't particularly relish the notion of seeing *Orange* destroyed before my eyes."

"I think you're being a little melodramatic," I counter. "*Orange* will be just fine."

"Right, it's only the first-ever and possibly last-ever Run Amok issue that you're ruining." She whips her hair out of the bun, brushes it crossly. "Really, Babylon, have you given any thought to what Izzie might do?" Her voice is thin yet strong, a wire. "The magazine has an articles inventory — Izzie could get the adult editors to pull a couple of all-nighters and basically waste everything we've done." She twists her hair again, twists it so tight the skin across her temples threatens to burst. "She could do that . . . she could . . . and Izzie . . . there's just no telling how malevolent she really is!"

Aha! "So you believe me about Izzie?" I demand.

"Believe you, Babylon?" Emmalee's eyes are hot blue flames. "I knew it before you did, knew it the instant I laid eyes on her in person — I got this ripple, this crawly sensation like a cobra had slithered into the room. But I couldn't *say* anything — Izzie LaPointe, revered by Run Amoks and girls with juice everywhere — so I hushed it, locked it up, played along. Because I cared about what we were doing. Even when Izzie would force her own agenda onto our stories, I believed that the core message to the readers was still intact. Maybe I was deluding myself. Maybe I just wanted to believe. . . ."

I sit on my bed, close to the dressing table, struck by this girl so easy to write off as cold and removed, who actually has more heart and soul than any of us. Emmalee subjugated her own feelings so we could achieve — not just us Run Amoks but all the *Orange* readers who wanted to *be* us, who could be us next year, or the year after. All I can think to say as her truth unfurls is, "Ohhh, Emmalee . . ."

"I should have confided in you, Babylon," she says. "There I was, mad at you when you didn't tell me you kissed Gabe. And I wanted to. But I — I was afraid. You mean so much to me, and I thought if I said anything against Izzie you'd shut me out. And now . . . " she trails off.

"Now?" I say. "Now don't worry. Emmalee, please. Izzie won't be happy but from what I've gleaned about her M.O., she's not about to trash the Run Amok issue. It's too high-profile; to scrap it would mean copping to a big fat failure. If anything, she'll replace the Think! section, but I don't think she will. I think she'll suck it up and run 'Girls vs. Girls' and take credit for the enormous success the Readers Run Amok program is bound to be."

Spontaneously, we reach for each other and hug. "It'll be all right, Emmalee, whatever happens," I say.

"I don't know; I still don't think you should go through with it, I really don't," she tells me. "But as long as our friendship survives, that's what matters most."

"I'll always be your friend, Em," I say. "You don't know how sick I felt the last few days, not sure if you were mad at me or what. I would've said something, if it weren't for all the work. . . ."

That word — work — makes us both sit back and stare at each other.

"You better get dressed," I deadpan. "We don't want to be late."

Five Run Amoks and their five mentors merge into the Kult Ink conference room at eleven sharp, Paulina laden with 11x17 sheets representing the fruits of our labors — page proofs of all the features for the December issue of *Orange*. There's a tangible tension in the air — we all know what's at stake here. The editors who guided us the last two months have as much invested in the outcome as we do. If Izzie's displeased by what we've wrought, she could go all *Alice in Wonderland* Queen of Hearts on them, offing heads at will. As to the Run Amoks, they know what's about to go down, and no matter what side they're on — for me, against me, or ambivalent — they've got to be curious about how it's going to play.

I sit with Natalie on my right, Emmalee to my left. Only Berni O'Rourke remains standing at the head of the table. "Wow, you guys!" she twitters merrily. "Wow, what with getting to know all of you, and seeing your progress, and me landing this huge promotion, this has just been the best summer ever!" She clasps her hands in front of her chest and displays a set of pearly whites marred slightly by a slip of lipstick. "Wow, I can hardly believe it's almost over!"

Is she really repeating "wow" that much, or is that the way she hiccups? I wonder.

"Izzie's been unavoidably detained, but she's on her way," Berni says. "Meantime I thought I'd give you the details about the fabulous event we're doing for you on Monday at The Pinnacle." Berni babbles on about the fancy luncheon that will mark the culmination of the Run Amok program. I tune her out — something tells me I won't be in attendance. I'm dangerously close to falling asleep when Izzie walks in, and adrenaline courses through me as if injected straight to my heart. What's more, Kult Ink president Alden Beck is with her — I had no idea he was coming to the meeting, but it makes sense that he'd want to see the results of Izzie's master plan.

"Sor-reee," Izzie singsongs, slinging her purse onto the table. Berni shuts up mid-sentence and takes her place next to Tabby. "Now don't feel you have to be on your best behavior because Alden's here. He knows how badass you are!"

Alden strolls to the back of the room and stands at the foot of the table. He's wearing a charcoal-gray suit today — must be visiting some advertisers later — and the sight of him so businesslike makes me check my posture. "Good morning, Run Amoks!" His voice is sonorous, the voice of someone accustomed to giving speeches, as he lets his eyes rest on each of us briefly. "I'm sure this is a bittersweet meeting for the *Orange* editors — next week, when you girls go home, they'll have to stop goofing off!" We all smile and giggle accordingly as he takes a seat. "I'm excited to see what you've come up with. Izzie, proceed!"

Izzie beams. "I hope Berni was getting you guys psyched about Monday, but she better not have spilled about the special guest I snagged to serenade us!" she says. "All I'll say is they better give lots of extra napkins because you guys will be droooo-ling." She sits, pulls her Sidekick from her bag, and studies it for a second. "But first things first, right? Paulina, what have you got for me?"

Paulina picks up the Stun! proofs from her stack. Izzie examines "Every Girl Is Beautiful" and "Come As You Are" quietly, thoughtfully, stroking her chin, almost like an actress playing an E-i-C in a movie. "I like!" she declares. "I like a lot. Beautiful work, Emmalee — even the captions, so cute!"

And so it goes. I know Paulina has the Think! proofs on

the bottom of the stack — it makes sense to get everyone else out of the way before all hell breaks loose. Izzie makes only the smallest changes on the proofs, tiny tweaks that allow her to impress upon us that she is the boss, and the boss knows best. Mostly it's kudos all around, and with every phrase of praise heaped upon the Run Amoks, I feel myself flip-flopping between pure resolve and complete regret.

"Last but definitely not least, Think!" Izzie says, aiming laser eyes on me. "My spies tell me you've been burning the midnight oil, Babylon, and I want you to know how much I admire that kind of work ethic. I know I'm going to love what you've done."

Soon as she lowers her gaze to the pages, the facial contortions begin. First a tic in her cheek, then a crinkle in her forehead, then a frown. All I feel is release. Not sated or avenged, but not empty or rueful either. Just this strange serenity. Basically the opposite of Izzie's emotional state as her fingers flip through the pages, searching for something that isn't there.

"What the? What is . . . this isn't . . ." Izzie's hands curl like claws around the proofs. But suddenly she smiles wide, cocks her head. "Okay, where's Ashton? I know when I've been punk'd!"

Ah, she thinks it's a prank. A logical conclusion, but no. As I rise from the table, Natalie gives my hand an encouraging squeeze. It's face-off time, for real.

"I'd like to explain what you're looking at, Izzie," I say. "One of the most invaluable lessons I learned this summer is how important it is to take risks. So although you approved a different story, I really believed this one to be newsier, smarter, more what *Orange* readers would want to know."

"Babylon, please — are you trying to tell me this . . . this . . ." Izzie lifts a corner of the page proof and drops it like it's diseased. "This is what you expect to go to press?"

I keep my eyes on Izzie's. "That's right," I say. "I had to go with my gut."

Izzie hacks up a harsh little laugh. "Ooh, guess you need some Pepto!" Someone giggles, but Izzie scrunches up her face in a show of sympathy. "It looks like you made one of your notorious Babylon bloopers! But of course that's understandable, you're only a child." She stabs her stare into my mentor. "You're the one I hold responsible, Natalie."

A lump the size of a softball lodges in my gullet as my ally is called onto the carpet. Watching this won't be easy.

"Yes, Izzie, I *am* responsible." Natalie's casual aplomb tells me she can handle it. "I can't take credit for the idea — that's pure Babylon — but I sanctioned it. We were confident that once you read the proofs, you'd realize it's the superior piece."

"I see, I see," says Izzie, her tone remarkably even for someone who looks like she just drank Drano. "I see that Think! has lost the ability to think straight."

235

Another giggle — Berni, I bet — but Izzie's attention is riveted on me. "Babylon, what I don't understand is why you didn't come to me if you were having problems with the assignment," she says. "My door is always open. So while I can appreciate the force of a young girl's impetuosity, I'm simply astounded that you took it this far. It shows very, very, very poor judgment. And I'll have you know I'm going to have to do some serious thinking between now and Monday — maybe I shouldn't be saying this, but you were among the top contenders for next year's Run Amok column, Babylon. You were so close . . . but now . . . I just don't know."

Okay, now I'm angry. Now I want to wipe that smug expression off Izzie's lying face with the sole of my sneaker. "Was I really close, Izzie?" I ask. "Because what you said about your door being open? Well, I don't know about always, but I know it was open on at least one occasion last week, when you were telling Berni and Marguerite that you'd picked me for the column before I even got here."

Gasps now, from Berni and Marguerite, surely, and some other senior staffers too.

"Excuse me?" Izzie's chair must be hot; she springs up. "You were *spying* on me?"

"No, I was helping Matumba, who was freaking out because she forgot to fetch your dry cleaning."

Suddenly Izzie catches her misstep — she lashed out at me for eavesdropping instead of denying my assertion. Her focus falters as she remembers Alden's presence in the room, and as she scrambles for a backtrack strategy, I drive it home. "And I also heard you say *why* you'd chosen me — you want me to be your biracial mascot, your 'in' with . . . what did you call it?" I pull out the words I'll never forget: " 'A population growing like mad yet in desperate need of a voice, a venue, a community.' "

The quote hits Izzie like a rotten egg. She literally passes a hand over her face, as if to wipe off the insult. "You're a lucky girl, Babylon." Her voice is like syrup. "Lucky that you're just a girl, a carefree little girl, playing at publishing. If you were an adult you'd have committed professional suicide. But I won't stoop to even acknowledge your ridiculous accusation. Nor will I take the time or energy to ruin you with every college admissions office in the country. I'm sure you'll continue to sabotage yourself repeatedly along the way, and I wouldn't be surprised to find you asking me to 'supersize that?' at some point in the future. All I'm going to do is ask you to sit down. Now. Please."

I can't believe she doesn't throw me out of the room — throw me out the window, me and Natalie both. Maybe it will be okay. Izzie's hopping mad, but it looks like, best-case scenario, she's going to eat it. So I shut my mouth and sit my ass down, as requested.

"Now, Paulina," Izzie says, "will you show me the page proofs for 'Girls Helping Girls' please?"

Paulina rises, but instead of saying, "There aren't any," she says, "Right here, Izzie," and moves to the head of the table, carrying a final stack of 11x17s. Next to me, Emmalee inhales sharply — she's thinking the same thing: How could I have believed Paulina would destroy the computer files? How could I have trusted her? Bitch doesn't even know the meaning of the word. She wanted the pleasure of watching Izzie squirm, but no way in hell was she about to put her neck on the chopping block.

Before Izzie examines the pages, she frames Paulina in her sights. "By the way, Paulina, I know Babylon couldn't have managed her master plan without you — your fingerprints are all over that fiasco!"

Paulina grins slyly. "You got me, Izzie," she says. "But I'm like you. I thought it was a joke, a stunt. Never in a million years did I think Babyl would actually try to stick it to you. After all you've done for her, for us, all of us. That's just psycho!"

Izzie seems convinced — she sniffs and quickly appraises the proofs. "These look fine," she says. "And although there's a small part of me that wants to strip your byline off these pages, Babylon, I'm going to let it go. I'm not going to be petty. That's just not the kind of person I am."

Oh, I know exactly what kind of person you are, I think to myself. But I keep my mouth shut. I sit there, mum and numb, while Izzie slips back into dazzle mode to wrap up the meeting and dismiss us. I rise like everyone else and begin to file out of the room. Right behind me, I can feel the stature of Alden Beck, who pauses at the head of the table. "Izzie?" he says. "I'd like a word with you."

FUN WITH THE FUTURE!

Consult the stars, read the tarot, decode the coffee grinds. There's a whole lot of adventure in store for girls with juice — but as to the particulars, who knows?

Only when we're back in Think! does Natalie give me a nod. "Well done," she says, extending her hand.

We shake. "Yeah, except I probably got you fired." Every action has a consequence; I'd hate for mine to turn Natalie into a bag lady. But she's cool.

"No worries, Babylon," she assures me. "Best thing that could happen. Because first of all, I was offered a gig at *Glamour* —"

"*Glamour*? Natalie, that's awesome!"

"You think? I don't know. Could be worse — could be *Cosmo*. Articles editor, that's the title, and the money's better than I'm making here." Natalie's fingers wander across the desk. "The problem is, a magazine for women my age, it's all about their sex life, their career . . . pointless, really. Not like here. Perhaps I suffer from arrested development, but I feel

240

like I belong in the teenage milieu. Like I'm having some impact, making a difference, steering girls toward smart decisions." She tucks her hair behind an ear, what I've come to recognize as a contemplative gesture. "So I haven't given *Glamour* my answer yet, since if Izzie does can me, I can collect unemployment and maybe pick up my novel again, or start a new one. Anyway, I have options — and that's a good feeling."

Listening to Natalie, a technical grown-up about to start over, I realize there's no such thing as a grown-up, that life is full of new directions, and whenever you head off in one, you're a child again. "Well, whatever you do, I know you'll be great," I say.

"Thanks, Babylon. So you want to grab a slice?" That's so Natalie. Pizza, the panacea.

"I would, but . . . the truth is I was up all night. Final throw-down in the Dorm of Doom." I look away from her. "I think I'm just going to blow off the rest of the day, if that's okay."

When I look back, Natalie's the one studying a spot on the wall. "Sure, sure." Quickly, she glances my way again. "You're not coming back, are you?"

I shake my head.

"I had a feeling. But you'll give me all your pertinent data — home address, phone, e-mail, et cetera?" Natalie grabs a pen and pad from her . . . our . . . someone's desk, scribbles all the ways to get in touch with her, and I, a beat behind, do the same. We exchange.

"Do I get a hug?" she asks.

"Try and stop me!" I say. "I just hope I'll be able to let go."

For a skinny woman, she sure is strong, and as we cling to each other I will best wishes into her. I also hope she really is what she represents: one of the good ones. Have I found a friend and mentor for life? I think so. But you never know.

Natalie hustles out after that, and I think she might be a little weepy. I would be, but I'm too tired for tears. I sit at my desk, check my e-mail. One message:

g.kandleman@squawk.com: pick u up @ 7. toothbrush suggested.

Hmm, Gabe and I have waited so long for our first real date, he's looking to make it a marathon.

b.edison@orange.com: are you abducting me?

He must've been waiting for my reply, because my in-box dings an instant later.

g.kandleman@squawk.com: ;)

A bed in an empty suite beckons, and I succumb, falling into a coma with my sneakers still on. When I regain consciousness, it's to a box of those crack-frosted cupcakes and my four suite mates crammed in the room.

"We couldn't decide between a Pulitzer Prize and an Academy Award, so we went for sugar instead," says Nae-Jo, plopping down next to me as I groggily get vertical.

Emmalee sits on the floor, proffers the box. "Your favorites," she says.

I indulge — peanut butter chip. "I accept this cupcake in the name of the Run Amoks!" I raise it aloft, then take a bite. "Damn, I'm going to miss these. They got to open a Treat Me Nice in Boston."

Mentioning my hometown is like banging a gong, reminding everyone of the imminent demise of our guild. My departure's just a bit more imminent than anyone else's. Emmalee rests her head against my leg and sighs. Paulina, who's gotten comfortable on Emmalee's bed, plucks at the lace trim on a pillow and says nothing. But Tabby selects a cupcake and tries to be cheerful. Clueless, but cheerful. "Well, we still have a few more days in NYC," she says. "And of course the luncheon at The Pinnacle! I wonder what special musical guest Izzie's got up her sleeve?"

Emmalee looks at me hopefully. Alas, I must disappoint. "Guys, I won't be going to The Pinnacle," I say. "It wouldn't be appropriate under the circumstances."

"Hey, I don't blame you," says Nae-Jo. "I mean, it'll probably just be bad rubber chicken."

I opt to make light of the situation. "Bad Rubber Chicken! I heard of them, some frat-rock band, right? You think that's the musical guest?" Giggles in harmony all around, and I seize on each one individually, like for a sonic scrapbook. "It'll be good to get home," I say earnestly. "See my folks, my friends. Jordan — get that all straightened out. I'm not . . ." How should I say this? "I'm not upset about the way things turned out, really. I wouldn't trade this experience for any-thing. And I know whichever one of you gets the column next year, you're going to make it amazing."

Stuffing the rest of the cupcake in my mouth, I spring off the bed, start fishing through the dresser for clothes for tonight . . . and tomorrow. The last thing I want is a big mushy scene with them right now. "Gabe will be here soon; I kind of need to get ready," I hint. The Run Amoks seem relieved to keep the maudlin to a minimum, too, and begin filing out. Only Emmalee throws a stormy glare toward Paulina, still stretched out indolently on Em's bed. She's in no rush to leave.

"Excuse me?" from Em.

"You're excused," from Paulina.

Time for me to step in. "Give us a minute, will you, Em?" I ask. Reluctantly she recedes. I toss an armful of underwear and T-shirts on my bed and turn to Paulina. "What?" I say to her.

"You hate me?"

Why would a creature like her even care?

"No, Paulina. I don't hate anyone."

"Good. Because I don't hate you. I mean, I screwed you over, sure — but not because I hate you. I just wasn't about to cut off my nose to spite my face, or whatever the cliché is. By any means necessary and all that."

She is *not* quoting Malcom X to me!

"I like you, Babylon, I actually do," Paulina continues. "You're funny, and you're not full of shit. And I *love* what you did to Izzie. That was paramount. Priceless. Glad I got to see it." That signature twisted twinkle. "Preserve it for posterity . . . "

"What are you talking about?" I'm not sure I want to know.

"Caught the whole scene on my Elura — tiniest camcorder going. Everyone was so fixated on you and Izzie, they wouldn't have noticed if I had a baby hippo in my lap." Paulina drops her long legs over the side of Emmalee's bed, pushes herself up. "Who knows when something like that may come in handy?"

In terms of pure, unmitigated evil, Izzie LaPointe is an amateur compared to Paulina Locke. "So I guess congratulations are in order," I say. "That column's going to be yours one way or the other."

"Seems that way," she says.

I find it hard to take my eyes off her. Tall frame, small eyes, electric hair. So that's what a sociopath looks like. Paulina ambles toward the door, leans against the jamb. "I'm glad we talked," she tells me. "But I knew you'd be cool. No one understands the killer instinct like you, Babylon."

Creepy. Creepy . . . but true.

THE FINE ART
OF FAREWELL

Saying good-bye to a great guy, your best friend, even a place you've come to love is so hard! Instead, go for a simple, sincere "see ya!"

When Gabe said he'd pick me up, I didn't know he meant it literally. Having packed my backpack with necessities, I leave the suddenly stultifying dorm to wait for him outside. Right on time, up pulls this Dadmobile — my date in the driver's seat. Gabe jumps out, puts his arms around me, and lifts me off the sidewalk, swings me around. Then he opens the passenger side. "Get in," he demands gruffly, tone borrowed from some old film noir.

He sits behind the wheel and gives me a look copped from the same fifties movie. "Consider yourself kidnapped," he says.

I giggle. "In a Buick Lucerne?"

Letting his sunglasses fall back in place, he pulls away from the curb, heads west. "Very funny."

"Where are we going?" I ask.

"Maple Hill," he tells me. "That's in New Jersey. That's where I'm from."

I remember the sunset Gabe and I shared out on the yacht, when he explained what made the colors so psychedelic. "Oh, really?"

"That's right," he says. "I want us to have a real first date, and to me that involves a parental encounter. Since I can't meet yours at the moment, you'll have to meet mine."

And they're so nice! So are his younger sisters — Tilly, who's thirteen and just back from camp, and Lucinda, who's my age and does all kinds of crafts, knitting and candle-making, stuff like that. Maple Hill is really nice too — a nice, normal, middle-class suburb with modest houses and neat front lawns and an ice-cream truck with a bell, winding its way through the neighborhood. I don't remind Gabe that he called New Jersey the Armpit of America.

He takes me to a French bistro in town and I show off by ordering *en francais*. Then on to hang out at a friend's — I flash on chez Quinn, up in Southie, and wonder if they're knocking 'em back there tonight. This is a small gathering, though, ten or twelve people, sitting around. Karaoke is suggested, and everyone's game. Some kids brought six-packs, but Gabe doesn't partake — he's driving — and I abstain too. Sobriety doesn't prevent me from delivering an inspired performance of "All Over Oliver." Gabe does "I Walk the Line" by Johnny Cash, his voice going way down low.

It's the most ordinary, regular, everyday night I've had in two months, and I love every minute of it. We don't stay at the party long, but we don't go straight home either. Gabe drives around, pointing out landmarks of his formative years — the hockey rink where he broke a tooth, the park that was overtaken by migrating Canadian geese who decided to stay for good. "It's a beautiful spot, and I'd take you for a walk — if it weren't for all the goose poop," Gabe tells me as he pulls into the parking lot. New York feels a million miles away, not merely across the river.

We sit and talk, which is so easy. Gabe knows how to listen, and if I'm ever at a loss for words, I can tap that impressive vocabulary of his. I even tell him about Jordan, and he's cool about it, understanding that I had a life before New York. "Jordan told me I'd changed," I say, summing up. "He was right. That's half the problem. The other half is he hadn't . . . probably never will. Although the truth is, I know I've changed — in that I've learned, I've grown. But I haven't really changed at all. Who I am, what I value. Not one iota."

"Given a chance he'll be able to see that," Gabe says. "Not that I'm encouraging you to give him that chance. In fact, if you never saw or spoke to him again, I'd be perfectly okay with that."

I lean my head against his arm and keep my focus straight ahead, flutters tickling me from the inside. I know Gabe is observing me in that way he has, the sweet-tart smirk-smile is on his lips. A similar expression steals over me, signifying a perception of the world as funny, nutty, wonderful, painful, all tumbling together at once. "I'll keep that in mind," I tell him eventually.

"Keep this in mind too." He turns me toward him with the whole length of his arm, leans his forehead against mine, watching me watching him in the just-enough-light, waits until neither one of us can wait anymore, and kisses me. From there, we proceed to a series of kisses in sometimes rapid, sometimes leisurely, succession, fulfilling a promise never quite made.

Dreamless and deep, I sleep on an air mattress in the Kandleman den, then wake to a feast of a family breakfast. When I cannot manage another bite, I ask if I can use the phone. "It's long distance," I put in, and Gabe's parents shoo me back to the den where I can have privacy. What will I tell my mom and dad? Not too much over the phone, I decide — just that I'm coming back a few days early. They don't bombard me with an onslaught of questions, just say they'll meet me at the shuttle and can hardly wait to see me. All is cool.

Back at the Dorm of Doom, Emmalee helps me pack. Between thrift stores and flea markets, thanks a lot to Emmalee's discriminating eye, it seems like I've accumulated quite a few additional items during my stay. I pick up the vintage slip my favorite fashionista cut into a top and re-trimmed with new lace on the straps and hem.

"How am I going to fit all this stuff?" I moan.

Emmalee extends her hand. "Here, like this," she demonstrates. "Certain fabrics you can roll up; they won't wrinkle. That'll give you more room. Cotton, of course, you have to fold. And linen, well, whatever you do, it will need ironing. . . ."

She's trying to be perfunctory and precise, all business over my bags. Futile. She drops a pair of shorts onto the pile. "Oh, damn," she mutters, and when I look in her eyes I see twin blue lakes.

"You're going to cry," I say quietly.

"Yes, damn it, I am going to cry." She commences to do just that. I put my arm around her and we sit on her bed — mine is covered with clothes — and I let her sniffle for a moment or two.

"This is only the beginning of us," I tell her. "It feels like the end, but it's not. College is just around the corner; maybe we'll wind up at the same place."

"What are you thinking — Columbia, I suppose?" she says, a tiny upturn threatening her pout.

"Why do you say that?" Of course, I know why. "Hey, I'm pretty crazy about him, Em, but I'm not about to revolve my higher education around a guy." I drink in our room, nodding. "I have grown rather fond of these delightful environs though," I say, mock-haughty. "And NYU has a killer journalism department."

"Yes, and FIT is nearby," she says. "Although my mother is under the misconception that I'll be spending next year modeling in Milan and won't even bother with college apps. I really must set that woman straight before she gets too carried away."

Talking about the future dries Emmalee's eyes. And I know that her future and mine will meld, somehow, someway. She'll become a force of the runway, a design diva, the new Stella McCartney. And I . . . hmmm . . . a masthead honcho, wielding words on staff at some smart magazine? Or a freelancer, selecting assignments so I can write about what truly matters to me? Or maybe I'll hole up in some miniscule attic apartment in Brooklyn, wait tables by night and toil away on a novel by day. Anything can happen. And it probably will.

HEY, WHO'S THE NEW GIRL?

Meet the new E-i-C of Orange!

Okay, this is probably the weirdest way I've ever introduced myself to anyone — let alone a million-plus girls with juice. But, actually, you already know me. As the former Think! Editor at *Orange*, I've been here from the beginning. Only now I'm stepping up, waaaaay up, and it is an honor and a privilege to serve as Editor-in-Chief at the preeminent voice of female youth culture. I, Natalie Helperin, do solemnly swear to bring you the coolest, most relevant, and ass-kickingest magazine every single month. (Of course, we'll all miss founding editor Izzie LaPointe, who's moving on to pursue other projects.)

So . . . new year, new editor. Oh, don't worry: I'll be true to *Orange's* core DNA — which means we'll continue to bring you smart stories, must-know news about sports and entertainment, and the kind of fashion and beauty real girls can relate to. But you'll also see some changes. One that I'm super-excited about is "My Page," a new column to be written each month by one of the Run Amoks — those five amazing girls you met in our December issue. Babylon, Emmalee, Nae-Jo, Paulina, and Tabby were the first-ever winners of our Readers Run Amok contest, and they did such a fantastic job producing the December issue, I figured they deserve to share a page all their own. And you know what? So do you! Don't forget to enter this year's Readers Run Amok contest — if you win, you'll not only spend a summer in the city, creating your favorite magazine, but you and your co-Run Amoks will have your own column for the following year.

I hope you enjoy the January *Orange*. Let me know what you think!

It's all love —

Nat

Natalie Helperin
Editor-in-Chief

ORANGE

RUN AMOK MUSINGS

New Year's revelations from a girl with juice...

By Babylon Edison

Welcome to the January issue and the debut of MyPage, the Run Amok column. I'm so excited to be kicking things off I thought I'd throw down a few random thoughts on the beauty of beginnings.

1 Every single day is the start of something big. So go for it!

2 A new friendship is a sprout in your heart. You have to nurture it — give it light, give it love, give it the food and water of your time and attention — and it should grow into a tree that will shelter you for the rest of your life.

3 That boy you just started talking to? He's not going anywhere. I mean, even if he is,

technically, miles away, if he's not an astronaut about to colonize Mars, if he's on this planet, you two have tons of time. Anticipating a kiss is just as delicious as the kiss itself.

4   That boy who for whatever reason you're not kissing anymore? Say hello to your new best guy friend. Unless he was mean to you (there is no room in your life for an abusive person), he can still mean a lot to you. It may take a minute for you and him to get to that place, but if you were special to each other, eventually you will be again.

5   The future is dazzling. It's a miracle. It's a bitch. Plan for it, sure, but embrace its unpredictability. Don't just expect the unexpected; welcome it. That's what will make you who you're bound to be. Oh, the most important thing about the future? It . . . starts . . . right . . . now. . . .

Sex. Fame. Rock 'n Roll.

Four kids on the fast track to pop-rock superstardom reveal the unfiltered truth about the glamorous, backstabbing world of sudden celebrity.

Introducing . . .

The Voice Sweet, trusting Kendall sings like an angel — and is about to discover her devilish side.

The Body Rich, spoiled Wynn can't keep a beat to save her life. But with curves like that . . . who cares?

The Boss No-nonsense Stella is all confidence, attitude, style, and smarts. But her relationship with the band's manager makes her more vulnerable than she thinks.

The Boy A/B has got real talent. Now if only he can keep his mind on the music . . . instead of on the girls.

6X *Idolize this!*

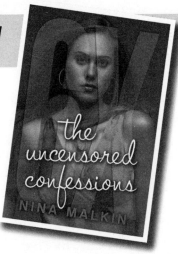

the uncensored confessions

NINA MALKIN

They call me The Body, though not to my face. Not that I would care. Maybe I would, I don't know. My mother says I should be proud of my body; she certainly is. I'm sorry, does that sound terrible? It's just that I read in a magazine about a girl my age who had a boob reduction — I mentioned that to my mom and she looked at me like I'd asked to be decapitated. Plus she's forever ordering me to stand up straight and put my shoulders back — a drill sergeant in socialite's clothing. When I started to develop, she would brag to her friends. Not that she actually takes credit for my body; in fact, she's always saying things like "It must be something in the water!" But that's how she thinks of me — as her creation.

Or her project. Because before 6X was anything, when it was just a crazy, this-will-never-happen-in-a-million-years idea, my mom was all for it. Not me. Even now, with our video on MTV ninety-seven times a day, it hasn't fully sunk in, since the way it started out was so unreal, so stupid. A big fat joke — with me as the punch line.

It was the holidays, and my stepdad's law firm was having a party at the Drake House, very fancy, all the lawyers and all the big clients. There was no reason for me to go — there wouldn't be any people my age, no kids to talk to — but my mother was like, "You're going."

So I went (you do not argue with my mother), and I swear, there is nothing more mind-numbing than watching a ballroom full of old people party. Waiters trudged around with trays of champagne and I thought: *Why not?* Nobody blinked when I took a glass. So I took another.

Sipping and walking, sipping and walking — that was my evening. Until all that sipping made walking kind of a challenge. I went to stand by the edge of the stage and watch the band, even though they were Top 40 — definitely not my thing. Soon as they took a break, the drummer came up to hit on me, which was *so* not appropriate. I mean, I'm a guest, and I'm fifteen. Anyway, I didn't know what to say — I'm pretty shy in general, and I get extra shy around guys who consider my boobs tantamount to the aurora borealis. But there I am — hello, little drunk girl — telling him how cool I thought it was that he played drums, because *I* always wanted to play drums — which wasn't true, I'd never even thought about it.

Next thing I know, he's leading me onto the stage and sitting me behind the kit and telling me what to do. I just start banging away, but within minutes my mom's unacceptable behavior radar picks up on my unacceptable behavior, and she dispatches my stepdad.

Only he's-not alone; he's with one of his partners, Brian Wandweilder — this entertainment lawyer, a real hotshot, the youngest partner at the firm.

"Well, well, well, Sherman," Mr. Wandweilder said to my stepdad. "I didn't know Wynnie played drums."

My stepdad smirked at him. "She doesn't," he said, then gave the drummer a dirty look and took my arm to help me down. I didn't complain; I was too busy babbling, "That was so much fun! Oh my God, that was SO FUN!" Such a ditz, I know — but the weird thing was Mr. Wandweilder kept going on about how incredible I was.

And later that night, in the limo coming home, my mom and stepdad were discussing it.

My stepdad was like: "And if you can believe it, Cynthia, Wandweilder actually said he could put a band together around Wynnie and sell it."

"Why wouldn't I believe it?" my mom said. She had that out-of-breath sound in her voice that she gets when she's irritated. "Wynn is a poised, beautiful, talented girl. And Brian knows the industry. You always say that. Do you think he was joking?"

"No, I actually think he *was* serious," my stepdad said, loosening his tie. "But he doesn't know Wynn. Really, Cynthia — can you envision our Wynnie bopping around onstage, playing drums in a rock band?"

They're having this conversation with me sitting between them in the limo. They're talking about me, and I'm sitting right there. And it's not like I'm passed out and drooling; I'm just a little drowsy.

"You're not denying that my daughter is poised and beautiful and talented, are you?" my mother said, raising an eyebrow in warning.

"Of course not," he replied quickly. "But Wynnie? In a band? Playing drums?"

"I simply think it might bring her out of her shell."

"Maybe," said my stepdad. He was quiet for a minute, mulling it over — he's like that, always looks at all the angles. "Maybe," he said again. "I just hope she doesn't come out of her *shirt*."

They call me The Voice. Oh gosh, no — not officially! That would be so rude. Because it's not like the other kids aren't talented. Because they are. Really. Just sometimes at Universe, our record label, they will say that. It's-kind of a slang thing in the industry to say "she's the voice" instead of "she's the lead singer." Anyway, singing-is what I do. Always has been.

Ask anyone in my family and they'll tell you about "The Nudge." We were all there in church — my mom and daddy, my grandparents, basically the whole town of Frog Level, South Carolina. And when the singing started, I opened my mouth like everyone else . . . and out it came. My voice. My mom says it was the sweetest, truest sound she ever heard — like an angel — but she had no idea it was little old me.

Well, once she realized it was *my* voice, she stopped singing herself and nudged my daddy with her elbow. He couldn't believe it either, so he nudged my granddad, next to him in the pew. And then it was like the wave — you know, the wave they do at football games? Like that. The Nudge started moving through the congregation until every last person, except for the preacher, got The Nudge and stopped singing and it was just me, three and a half years old, belting out "What a Friend We Have in Jesus" like nobody's business. It was my first solo.

Gosh, that's a back-home story for you. All my family is still down there in Frog Level. That old church isn't there anymore but I can remember it: white clapboard, wooden floor, and so tiny — standing room only on any given Sunday. Isn't memory strange? I think it is. Because even though I can remember that church, what I cannot remember, what I wish I *could* remember more than anything, is my daddy.

What happened was, he got killed defending our country in the Gulf War. And my mom doesn't have any pictures of him — they went missing because my mom and I moved around so much. After we lost my daddy, my mom had to work real hard at the Wal-Mart and go to college, but once she earned her degree she kept on looking for better and better jobs. And for some reason the better the job, the farther up North it was. She's got a wonderful position now; they love her. My mom is serious about her career; she is an *executive* at the top of middle management. It's one of the things that makes me so proud of her.

Anyway, all those pictures of my daddy. Lost. It's sad, I think, but I don't dwell on it, because I am a very positive person. Plus I know my daddy's up on a cloud, watching all the awesome things that are happening for me. Sometimes I like to think that when I sing, my daddy is starting a Nudge right there in heaven!

Look, no offense but it's dumb to try to label the members of this band. Back in the boy-band era maybe that's what they did — he's the poet, he's the bad boy, he's the sex god — but please, that is over. It's just stereotyping, which I am personally very much against, and which our band is so not about. Because check it out, here's the black girl and she's not in-an R&B group and she's not even the singer. Our band is about breaking barriers.

But whatever, if these video diaries get turned into a reality show or some kind of special-bonus-extra content for our CD, and that helps sell records — cool. See, that's how my mind works. I am a businesswoman. First and foremost. And an artist. An artist and a businesswoman.

I make shit happen. Like that day in school, when Wynn first brought up the band thing in homeroom. We both go to Little Red Schoolhouse. Yes, that is really the name of our school — so cute I could vomit.

Back in the day, Wynn wasn't exactly a friend, but we had a few classes together, we talked. Well, one time she's telling me about some chichi champagne-fueled night out, and this drummer dude who's clearly trying to find a way into her thong. I'm half-listening to this shit, but the second she gets to the part about her step-dad's law partner claiming he could build a band around her, I-snap to. I mean, I'm riveted. Right away, I'm like: "Really? I play bass."

And that weekend, I learned how.

That's where Loserboy came in. Twenty-five years old, can't even hold a job at the freakin' post office . . . pathetic. But I love him like crazy, he's my big brother, all right. So he's got this bass (he was in a band for five minutes once), and that Friday night we put on the Ramones' *Leave Home* and *Rocket to Russia* — old-school punk is one of the few things me and JJ have in common — and I strap on his big-ass Fender P. It comes down below my knees and looks retarded, but he teaches me a couple of bass lines and all weekend I practice. The next Monday at school I'm all over Wynn about the band, the band, the band.

And if that makes me pushy or aggressive or a bitch then, fine, whatever. . . .

The Boy

Ah yes: The Boy. The dude, the guy, the Y chromosome. That's me. Most of all, though, I'm the musician. Every band's gotta have at least one. Not to be a complete asshole but hey, we've all got our jobs.

Wynn's job is to be the babe. Oh, she keeps the beat okay — believe me, when I first heard her I was like "no way," but it's amazing how much she's improved. Only come on, calling her "attractive" is like saying the Grand Canyon is a hole in the ground. She could be up there hitting a bucket with a pair of knitting needles and people would still shell out twenty bucks to watch her. As for Stella, she's also a graduate of the leaps-and-bounds improvement program. Still, playing bass is not her main thing. Hmm, how can I put this? Stella's job is to be the boss. We've got a manager and an A&R guy and a lawyer and a label, but Stella's the boss because she scares the crap out of us. The girl was a Mafia kingpin or a Third World dictator in a former life, I shit you not.

Kendall, obviously, her job is to sing. She's one of those people, you hand them the phone book and when they start singing it, your jaw drops, you get goose bumps, the whole nine. So you could say that Kendall's a musician, too, but I beg to differ. She's something else: a natural. Never took a lesson. Pure gift. Me, I got some gift action going — at the risk of coming off completely obnoxious, I *can* play anything — but while Kendall just does it, I have to work at it. Only it's not work, because I love it.

I was eleven in my first band, a cover band, classic rock. Everyone else was in their late twenties and thirties. I was the gimmick, the little piano prodigy. By age thirteen I'd switched to guitar as my main instrument and started a band with some kids on my block. Here's the rest of my musical résumé to date: I had a ska-punk band; an emo band; a very strange duo with this guy from camp — me on guitar and keyboards and him on oboe and flute; your basic generic rock band; a very short-lived nu-metal thing; and two things I can only categorize with the meaningless tag of "indie rock." Where did they all go? Nowhere.

So about a year or so ago, I started doing the coffee-house open-mike circuit. Just me and my six-string soul mate doing a set of obscure covers and crappy originals. Yet somehow that's how I hooked up with a manager, and through him I met this guy who knew a lawyer who hooked me up with the girls, and now we're 6X, pop-rock sensation, superstars in training.

Does that sound simple as A-B-C? One-two-three? Vini, vidi, vici? Yeah, right . . .

To Do List: Read all the Point books!

By Aimee Friedman

❏ **South Beach**
0-439-70678-5

❏ **French Kiss**
0-439-79281-9

❏ **Hollywood Hills**
0-439-79282-7

By Hailey Abbott

❏ **Summer Boys**
0-439-54020-8

❏ **Next Summer: A Summer Boys Novel**
0-439-75540-9

❏ **After Summer: A Summer Boys Novel**
0-439-86367-8

❏ **Last Summer: A Summer Boys Novel**
0-439-86725-8

By Claudia Gabel

❏ **In or Out**
0-439-91853-7

By Nina Malkin

❏ **6X: The Uncensored Confessions**
0-439-72421-X

❏ **6X: Loud, Fast, & Out of Control**
0-439-72422-8

❏ **Orange Is the New Pink**
0-439-89965-6

Point

POINTCKLT